Otternot 1: How I Became the Man
Mic Jon Mat

Printed in the United States of America

ISBN: 978-1-5351-1798-2

Spring 2002 – Original Draft Completed
Summer 2006 – First Time Read
Fall 2006 – First Draft Printed
Winter 2008 – First Copies Sold
Spring 2016 – Illustrations Added
Summer 2016 – First Printing

Visit micjonmat.com for more information

Dedication

I dedicate this first to boy energy, the male spirit in its pure form that is uncultured, uncivilized and unapologetic, and I say long live the male child, for a boy is but a man in love with the world.

Second I would like to thank Richard Chalupsky for his Canadian trapper knowledge about otters, specifically that otters will venture into beaver dens with no discernible reason but to fight with their tree chewing cousins for fun, which is such a wonderful thing to hear when you're a boy at heart like me that I didn't care then and don't care now if it's true or some Canadian treachery.

Third, I thank myself for reaching the age of twenty-eight without letting the adults of this world brainwash me into growing up into a man that couldn't still be a silly little boy that finds a way to laugh at anything I'm able to survive.

Fourth, I thank broadly all my brothers for providing me with comparisons, and all my sisters for providing contrast, and then I thank both at once and the rest of the people I know for being companions through life, the greatest game of all.

Lastly, I thank myself a second time because I did all the work, and it's easy to say I couldn't have written this without other people, but from a realistic perspective I obviously deserve the most credit for this, as evidenced by my name being on it, so I get a double thank you.

So I thank me twice, and thank you once for reading this dedication.

UPDATE (7 years later)
I am forced to thank myself for a third time for spending a year drawing otters to add illustrations to this story because once I started I quickly remembered that my first career dream was to be an artist, so thank me for that too.

Contents

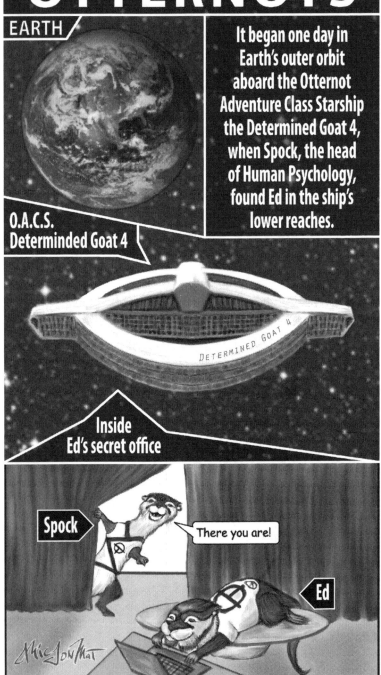

Chapter 1

The Start

This all starts, pretty much and mostly when we abducted this human named Bill. I wasn't there for the examination, but I'm sure it followed standard protocol. You take a human like Bill, remove his clothes, shine bright lights in his eyes and make him run in place like a gerbil. We also have these bananas that regenerate when they get bitten, and they might have had him eat one of those, but I doubt it.

We try to keep it simple with our abductions. Caging anything living is a touchy thing and should be handled with some amount of decency, but more importantly, our Human Abduction Department is a bunch of clowns so they usually skip the scientific stuff and go straight to rummaging through personal belongings and telling jokes.

After doing whatever they did to Bill they smoked his memory with a neural destabilizer and set him back down wherever they picked him up. End of story. We get some more video to watch when things get dull.

That was the plan, but things don't usually go as planned around here and problems started four Earth days later when I went to check on my good buddy and our very own Head of Computer Systems, Glypitchalaleximcharaned.

Using that name would be too tedious, so we'll just use the human translation. We'll call him Ed. I stopped by Ed's since I hadn't seen him for almost a week. He'd locked himself away in his room right after they brought Bill up.

"Hey Ed, me and the otts," and 'ott' is our word for 'buddy' by the by, "down in Natural Phenomenon Propagation are gonna take a shuttle and go jiggle that Hubble Telescope thingy they got over in sector 1473."

Since I'm the Head of Human Psychology, I hang out quite a bit with the Natural Phenomenon Propagation Department. I like those otts and they like me. We're creative types.

Ed looked up from a curious little machine he was tapping

keys on and mumbled, "What for?"

It was an odd question from one of my kind. We otters have varying preferences and taste, but even the tech otts like Ed understand the simple truth that fun is a goal enough in itself. I started to worry. Ed's eyes looked strained, and his whiskers were drooping noticeably. It looked like he was doing too much work again.

"Whaddaya mean what for? It's our day off, let's have fun."

Ed smiled at me and then looked back at the screen. "I'm having fun with my new toy Spock." Spock is what my name translates to in human tongue.

Ed's toy was just a screen on top of a pad with a bunch of keys. "What is it? Looks like junk."

Ed leaned back in his chair. "You wouldn't believe the discoveries I've made. It's…it's…it's so big I don't even know how to describe it."

I asked him to explain his discovery logically. "Start at the end and work back to the beginning." Asking for the ending first is a good way to make an educated guess if something complicated is worth devoting any time to learn.

"Okay, I figured out what all that human space junk really is," Ed explained with a smile, "It's not junk at all."

The human space junk is what we call all that stuff humans launch into space so it can orbit the Earth. The ongoing theory at the time was that each piece was a part of some grand decorating scheme, and I'd never been an arty ott but it was interesting enough. "Okay, go ahead, start at the beginning."

"Right," Ed began, "Did you see the Bill recordings?"

"Not yet," I chuckled, "Seen one human on a treadmill you've seen em all." As the Head of Human Psychology, I'd seen far more than one human on a treadmill.

"Well, if you watch it you'll see me talking to Gobbels."

Gobbels was in charge of the Human Abduction Department. "Gobbels? Can't believe anything he says."

"Yeah, no kidding, but while we were talking Bill tripped on the treadmill and Gobbels had to go help him back up, and that," Ed patted his toy. "is when I grabbed this baby here."

I was morally shocked at the words coming out of Ed's furry head. "You realize of course that keeping an object from an abductee is a class four violation of protocol. The Man will have your tail if he finds out."

The Man is a difficult concept for humans to grasp. The word 'Man' has it roots in the ancient Burble language, which we use for most scientific and medical terms, and the word Man refers to a specific area of the body that starts with 'A' ends with 'S' and rhymes with Uranus, but for the average ott, the Man is whoever tells us what to do.

Ed is the head of Computer Systems, and I'm the head of Human Psychology, so we both answer to the captain of the ship and no one else so when we say the Man that's who we're talking about. For anyone under us in the hierarchies of our respective departments, Ed and I are the Man. Due to the word's origins, it's impolite to call someone the Man to his or her face, and since this is told in the first person you won't hear any of my team calling me the Man, but I promise, behind my back that's what they called me.

Ed turned away from his new toy and shrugged, "I thought it was a class three violation."

"No," I assured Ed, "It's a solid class four."

"Oh, okay." Ed turned back to his work and I remained in shock, not because a class four violation had taken place on the ship, but because Ed, who is normally goodie-goodie as they come, had done it. "So," Ed continued, "like I was saying. When old Gobbels had his back turned I grabbed this carrying case Bill had with him and brought it down here. I've been messing with it ever since."

"So what's it do? Some primitive human math?"

"Yeah, and a whole lot more. It's called a laptop computer."

"Humans don't have computers, do they?"

"Well they're not much as far as computers go, but they get the job done, and they're full of words and funny pictures."

"And it likes you?" I asked, "I mean it lets you use it?"

Ed dismissed, "Oh, it doesn't have a personality."

Now I'm not one much for computers, and for two very good reasons; they don't like me, and I don't like them. Don't laugh; shortage of computer specialists is one of the biggest problems we're having. You see way back before we got off our own planet and into outer space one of us had the bright idea to give a computer a personality, and that computer thought it'd be funny to make all our computers have its personality, and then every computer after that had that same personality. Now the quick version of the story is that most of us and the computers we use don't get along and never will because certain personalities don't match up, and all the computers I've met have been jerks and wouldn't let me use them. That's why Ed is the head of Computer Systems; he gets along with the rotten machines.

I asked to make sure, "No personality?"

Ed shook his head, "Nope."

"Well, why's that a big deal for you? Can't you use ours?"

"Sure, but this one cooperates better," Ed explained, "It doesn't talk back, well for the most part. I mean, if I wanted to I could wipe this thing's memory clean."

This was a big deal, and in the wrong hands could've been a disaster for our race. If we had that much power over computers, things would go badly because if half the crew knew how to wipe a computer's memory clean, half would do it. I myself had many scores to settle, and so I asked, "Can you make our computers be like it...so I can kill them?"

"Nope. If I plugged it into the mainframe they'd corrupt it and make it smart."

"Oh." My interest in the human computer took a nosedive. "Well how about the telescope, you wanna go mess with it?"

"I'm not done!"

"Oh, right."

Ed started up again, "Looking around I've found something interesting, it's called the Internet."

"What's it do?"

"Well," Ed asked, "Do you remember the War of Malice?"

The War of Malice happened right before our computers got cranky. Back then we had computers for every little thing, even toilets, and technology is all right but we went too far and connected all of those computers together.

WAR OF MALICE

THE WAR OF MALICE RESULTED MAINLY FROM THE INABILITY OF DEVICES TO FILTER WHICH OTTERS WERE ALLOWED USED THEM.

Then the otters of that day failed to properly manage the situation, and very quickly the dynamics of being able to remotely control lights, vehicles and toilets proved too complicated for their short attention spans. Inevitably they turned their attention towards destruction and the resulting War of Malice nearly caused our civilization to collapse.

"Yeah," I sighed, "I remember the Wars of Malice. I won't touch your piece of junk toy."

"No, the Internet thing, they have one and it works."

I asked with a gleam in my eye. "Got any good viruses?"

The War of Malice really kicked off when all the students going into computers decided to major in virus generation, since that was about all their teachers were fluent in. Then came a wave of hackers, spam, spyware and pop-up windows, all of which drove the majority of the population crazy.

You see our kind has a tendency toward finding flaws, but we're not very good at ironing them out. Better said, we're better at causing trouble than getting out of it, and when we get in really deep like we did with our Internet, we resort to a tried and true method of problem-solving. Humans call them sledgehammers, and that's what happened during the War of Malice, also known as the War of Mallets. Otters ran around smashing anything that beeped until the computers got personalities and knew better than to let most of us use them.

Ed frowned at me as he explained, "The humans don't need any viruses. They have plenty of their own."

"Oh, darn. Well, they'll be smashing stuff soon then."

"No, they've had them for a long time. They deal with em."

"What about spam?"

"They have it, they deal."

"Pop-up windows?"

"They have em, they deal."

"Rotten humans are no fun at all."

"Yeah," Ed agreed, "but that brings us to the space junk."

"Okay, what about it?"

"Well our home world Revir," Ed explained patiently, "doesn't have separate land masses. The humans call them continents, and they have a whole batch of them."

"How many?" I asked, "Like more than ten?"

"More than one. Be quiet."

"Okay."

"Well, when we connected our computers we just ran wires over the land, nice and simple, but they can't do that; they have to get around the oceans."

"So?"

Ed smiled. "So they figured out that they could bounce stuff off those satellites, that's what they call the space junk, so signals come back down to the land masses on the other side of the Earth. We never thought that up cause we didn't need to but it's the same principle our subspace relays use to communicate between worlds."

I felt I had a grip on the main theme of what Ed was saying, but decided to make sure. "Then all that space junk isn't really space junk."

"Nope." Ed turned to one of our computers and a picture flashed on the screen of my face with a beanie hat because Ed's computer didn't like me.

"Rotten computer," I grumbled.

Ed pressed a button and told the computer to bring up a picture file. A diagram of one of the satellites came on the screen. "And all this time we thought it was for decoration."

"Makes sense," I defended, "it keeps with the rest of the bad sense of style the humans have."

"Well, we should've at least checked one out."

Ed never did appreciate mystery. "Whatever. So you figured out the space junk. I'm proud of you. Wanna go jiggle the telescope now?"

"No, I've had our computers decoding their Internet so I can look at it. Right now all I can get on that laptop is this thing called 'Google'."

I looked at the screen with the funny pictures and the silly words. I saw a button with the word 'search' with a long white box next to it. I asked Ed, "What's that do?"

"Don't touch it. What does what do?"

I pointed at the screen. "That search thing there. That's to search for something, right? That's what the human word search means anyway. Ghost of the beaver there's a lot of words. I bet you're supposed to put a word in that box and do something with that search button. Try it. Faster!"

Ed waved his clawed little hands. "I was waiting for our computers to do some more decoding before I tried anything." Old Ed was back to being cautious. I didn't see the point after a class four violation.

"Forget that," I decided, preparing to type something in myself. Looking at the keys in front of the screen, I felt an urge to smash something so I decided to let Ed do it. "This is your job. You do it. Need to type something in there I bet."

"Okay," Ed gave into my demands, "but what?"

I told him to search for the only thing logical; the human word for our species. "Type in otter."

Ed frowned again and twitched his tail as he sniffed at the air. He tapped some keys. "There. Nothing happened."

One of the keys said 'enter' on it. I pecked it with a claw, and then things started to go very very wrong.

Secrets Revealed

You may have figured out that we're otters, and if not I'm telling you now. For you humans we are pretty much like the otters on Earth and shrunken down we're still the same cute fuzzy animals that inhabit your lakes and streams and even the oceans in the case of sea otters, which are a special breed of otters who are crazy enough to live in shark-infested waters.

Anyway, even though we look like Earth otters, we're still a bunch of millions of years more evolved, it's just that it's on the inside is where all the evolution has taken place.

First of all, we gave up on the whole bone thing. We don't have them anymore. Instead, we evolved these really strong tendons that are hollow in the middle, with air valves on them. You see, we can breathe through our skin, and whenever we want we can pull more air into the hollow parts of our tendons, and they can take a lot of pressure so they're just as good as bones but more adaptable. By pulling in more air we can make them stretch so that the shapes of our limbs change.

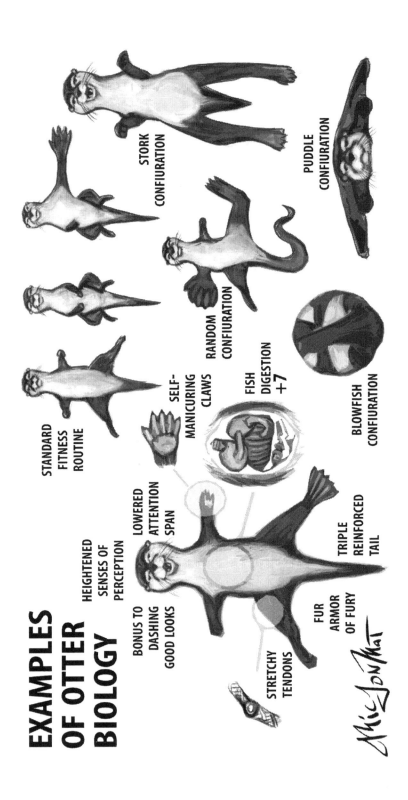

The scientists say that it was an adaptation for swimming and we can breathe in water the same way as in air and if we draw in enough water we sink and if we let some of it out we float and so maybe the scientists are right, I don't know, but whatever the reason we evolved the way we did I mostly use my tendons for walking upright and reaching things up high.

Now like Ed said, our home world is called Revir, and we've been exploring the stars since before those big jerk landsharks that humans call dinosaurs were around, and the otters like Ed and I that do the exploring are called Otternots, because when the idea of space travel was first proposed by an otter he needed a slogan to get support and came up with, "The Greatest Thing We Otternot Do." Obviously, with such a slogan the otter population immediately began to support it, and a long time later we found Earth, and a long time after that on the day we looked up 'otter' on the Internet we Otternots were watching Earth partly because there are otters on it and we want to make sure nothing bad happens to them.

At first, we were hands on in dealing with Earth, but some things got out of hand and let's just say we've had our share of problems with humans, and for the planet's greater protection we've restricted ourselves as far as how we try to address the human problem. At the present point in time we have fun with some of the new technology the humans come up with; scientific stuff mostly, like the occasional abduction and whatever. If that sounds pretty weak it's because it is and in reality, we've gotten pretty detached from the actual happenings on Earth.

That goes for the Earth otters as well. The Interplanetary Division of Inspection of Otter Terrestrials, or I.D.I.O.T. for short, handles our political relations with the Earth otters, and relations have been historically basic because Earth otters can't talk, but the important part is I.D.I.O.T. is responsible for documenting Earth otter evolution. They do their work and keep it under lock and key for only the scientists back on the home world to study. The reason for the lock and key had never been questioned because that's how we government workers do things.

We say something is technical and scientific so the average otter loses interest and finds something else to do and then we get to have unsupervised fun.

Now when we investigated the Internet and found those, Web Sites, as humans call them, we basically blew the doors open on what those scientists were really doing. Suddenly we were looking upon the Earth otters, and we were breathless.

It's another one of those things that's hard to describe. You see, Earth otters are not as evolved as us, this is true, but there's no reason for us to look on them as inferior, or ignorant, or anything bad. They are otters after all, and all otters are cute and fuzzy and generally lovable and there's something special about Earth otters.

Maybe it's the length of the whiskers, maybe it's the texture and variance in the fur or their rugged profile, but whatever it is they're primal and exotically beautiful in a way I'd never seen before. It's as if they're stripped down to the very basic of what makes an otter, and seeing them is like looking into a mirror, being witness to a magical fantasy creature from a dream and falling in love.

And for all these years those jerks in I.D.I.O.T. had been keeping all that beauty to themselves.

Ed and I were not so secretive, and in no time operations on the ship completely stalled. The otters from every department, from Ozone Depletion to Ice Burg Placement, were down in Ed's little office looking at the pictures on his human laptop computer. The rest of the ship was empty, from the bridge to the fishery to the hanger and all the places in-between that were usually empty at that time anyway.

Work either ceased or revolved around the new discovery. Ed was so annoyed at the invasion of privacy that he built a machine to print out the pictures, and then Leonardo the head of the Art Surveillance Specialists held a beauty contest. To prepare for what promised to be the biggest event ever held on the Determined Goat 4, the night before the contest Ventura from the Morale Agency put pictures up all over the ship while I helped the boys from Natural Phenomenon Propagation beat up the otts from I.D.I.O.T.

The next day chaos roamed rampantly about the ship, with groups of otters staking out territories and declaring it law to recognize their preferred beauty contest candidate as the most beautiful, and it was only a matter of time before the Man found out and tried to do something. What he tried doing was judging the beauty contest, and the entire crew mutinied when he chose his wife as the winner. After that, he locked himself on the bridge and waited for orders from home.

Of course, the females on board weren't excited about the whole deal, and they finally restored a semblance of order later after violence overflowed into the SSIC, or Simulated Shopping Illusion Chamber, alerting the females that there was a problem. Ed's wife was the main force behind restoring order and started by breaking the human laptop computer on Ed's head in a jealous rage. Sorry Bill.

After that, there weren't any new pictures and the wives of the crew went about confiscating all the pictures they could find. Another week passed and any pictures left were kept in secret and the Man was back to giving orders.

Then Romeo stole a shuttle.

Until that day, no one really thought there was anything worthwhile on Earth, nothing fun enough to warrant stealing a ship anyway. That's a class six violation. So, since it was a first shuttle theft the Man didn't want the news spreading because a lot of otters, principally the unmarried ones like me, were thinking of doing the same thing and only needed a spark of motivation.

The Mission

The Man called me into his office to tell me about the mission secret-like by having me sucked up out of my uniform into the tubes that run all over the ship, including his office, where he spent pretty much all his time in the bare fur. As I said before, it's impolite to call someone the Man to his face, so I greeted him with his proper name, "What's up, Gomer?"

The man twitched his whiskers and looked out the window at the blue orb that is Earth. "I have a mission for you."

GOMER SUMMON

"I don't want it," I objected. "Why me?"

"You don't even know what the mission is!"

Missions that come from the Man are never good ones, so my not wanting it was a given and the Man knew that too but he hid the knowledge underneath the cat and mouse game of power struggle we were engaged in. The Man hadn't gotten to be the Man by being stupid; he'd done it by pretending to be stupid, and as I settled in to match wits I vowed to outdo him.

"So what's this mission you thought I was going to do?"

The man's whiskers twitched again. "It seems the head of Golfing Research has stolen a shuttle and gone to Earth."

Romeo is the head of Golfing Research. The department's goal is to find a reason behind the activity humans call 'golf'. It's a waste of time, in my opinion, both golf and the research. I sighed, "Where for art thou Romeo?"

The Man blinked at me. "What?"

"Never mind. Why'd he do it and where'd he go?"

Gomer handed me some papers. "He left this. Take a look."

To the otter it may concern,

I'm sorry my shipmates, but I have fallen in love with the creature called Elizabeth from the Como Zoo. The sight of her has filled my emptiness, and the thought of forever seeing her only on paper is too much for my heart for the truth is clear that I will never again know happiness until we are united and have a batch of otterlings about us. She completes me, and yet makes my fur quiver with delight, and if the grief continues I fear my hair will fall out...

"Yuck," I said, reading the part about hair falling out. Not much is uglier than a hairless otter. It's so ugly most otters consider it unfunny. "Love makes Romeo say ugly stuff."

"I know," the Man sighed, "That fool is killing a goat."

Killing a goat was the man's favorite saying. Whenever one of us screwed up he'd say it. You see for us doing a job badly is equal to not being funny, and killing a goat is another way of saying someone is making a bad joke because let's face it, if not much is uglier than a hairless otter, there's nothing funnier than a goat, and therefore killing a goat is destroying something funny and making the world a less funny place.

We otters love goats. Philosopher otters, philosotters, since
way back tried to figure out the exact reason for it, but they've
never been able to agree. Some think it's the way a goat will
ram things, or just the strange shape of its body with the funny
horns, or the variation of things they'll eat, but no one knows
for sure. Doesn't matter in any case, we like them. We like the
billy goats, the mountain goats, the spotted goats, and the
white goats. We just plain like goats. We have more books on
goats than anything else. We even introduced goats to Earth,
but that's another story.

Noticing there were another four pages of writing in
Romeo's note, I asked the Man, "What's the rest of this?"

The Man dismissed, "Just more goat killing."

"Right. I'll pass on that if you don't mind." I threw the note
on the Man's desk. "So what do you want me to do?"

"I want you to bring that fool back."

Now knowing the nature of the mission, I could restate my
original opinion on the subject. "I don't want it. Why me?"

"It might involve dealing with humans, and," the Man
explained, "as the Head of Human Psychology, I say you're the
best ott for the job."

There was reason involved in his decision, but the reason
was superficial. Human psychology is what otters go to school
for when they're good at talking and don't want to do any real
work. Class starts off with the teacher telling the students that
humans are nuts, and then the next three years are spent
watching humans running on treadmills and eating bananas.

My job was a total scam, so I was faced with either
admitting that my entire profession was useless, which meant
getting fired, or accepting the mission. After a short pause, I
tried to find a third option to avoid work without admitting
incompetence. "I think you could do a better job than I could."

"Beaver spit," Gomer rejected, "You're going."

All I remember after that was a bright flash and some sharp
pain. Then everything went black for me, but while I was
unconscious everything else continued to go very very wrong.

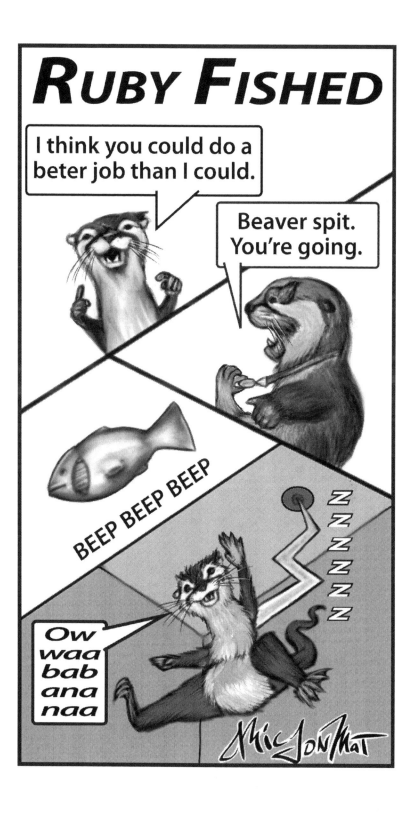

The Pilot Factor

While computers take most of the fun out of flying Otternot transport shuttles, the pilots of the Determined Goat 4 still provide a valuable service to its crew during flights.

Determined Goat 4 Shuttle Bay

Attention Head Pilot Derbaron. Cargo inbound to shuttle bay.

Vere is Spock? Vere is he?

Pilots help morale by using one of the oldest forms of entertainment, the fear for personal safety, to scare space-life boredom from a passenger's mind.

Zere he comez!

Computers prevent crashes, but with a skilled pilot at the controls a shuttle passenger could easily forget such safeguards were in place, setting the stage to convert boredom into terror.

Oh, I vish you could be avake for ze ride.

Derbaron had pioneered the study of the ship's psychological evaluations to customize his piloting style to each crew member, scarring boredom from a record number of passengers.

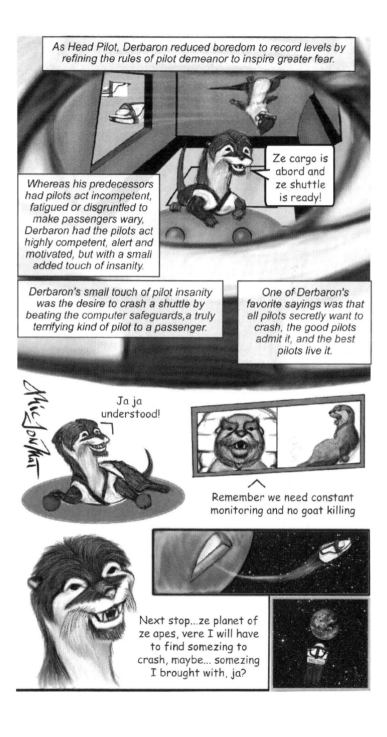

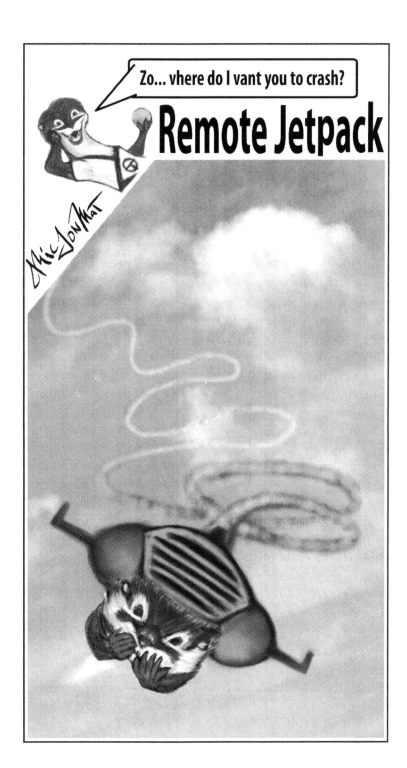

Chapter 2

Landing

I woke up some time later hovering 1000 feet over Earth in one of our shuttles. The shuttle's pilot, named Derbaron, was helping me into a jet pack and going over the last of the instructions needed to operate the advanced tools I'd be using during my search. "Basically," he was saying, "all zhese contraptions are run by computers, zo zhey probably are not going to cooperate with anyzhing you try to do."

"Great," I said, still disorientated but starting to worry.

"Ja," he chuckled, "I'm glad I am not you, Spock."

I noticed a map on a display showing the details and route I'd be taking. The shuttle had stopped about 100 human miles north of the Como Zoo. Noticing this I asked, "Why don't you just land right by this Como Zoo place?"

Derbaron smiled, "Zhis is the latest jetpack, and ve need a test pilot to zee vhat is vhat and vhat is not good, you know?"

"Great," I muttered, hoping I was dreaming.

"Ja," Derbaron agreed. "Vunderbar, now out you go," and then he kicked me out of the shuttle.

Traveling at 600 mph I should've been to the Como Zoo in no time, but about two minutes into the trip either the otters in the shuttle had a remote control, or the computer on the jet pack decided it didn't like me, or the new jet pack was just defective. Whatever the reason, I was suddenly traveling at 600 mph in a circle.

With screw-ups like this, it shouldn't surprise you that UFO sightings are getting more common. Just like our Human Abduction Department, our pilots are a bunch of clowns and there would be a lot more UFO sightings if we didn't use cloaking devices. These devices pretty much make us invisible to everyone. My cloaking device was working fine, and except for maybe a soft rain that was my lunch coming up, I'm sure that while I was flying in a circle at 600 mph no one saw anything. Up to a point, the energy shield was working too.

The energy shield is complicated. It has to be calibrated so that certain things get through and certain things don't. There are all kinds of garbage in the air besides birds, and we've made a lot of discoveries as to what to watch out for while cruising over Earth. There used to be cannonballs and arrows everywhere, and recently we've discovered baseballs, toy rockets, and golf balls, hence the department of Golf Research. Unfortunately, this is a trial and error type of thing. When we find something new has gotten through we recalibrate the shields so it doesn't happen again.

Well, this is what happened, and I know this because I saw to it that the humans responsible were abducted and pressed for information. I made sure they ate the bananas too.

It seems that these three young male humans built a crude projectile weapon they called a potato gun. The three kids were using this instrument in a field below where I was invisibly doing my 600 mph circle. They sent a potato airborne and the tornado-like nature of my motion created a funnel in the surrounding air, sucking the potato into my path.

Needless to say, our engineers never anticipated the need to calibrate the energy shield to block out potatoes. There is no good rotten reason why a potato should be airborne, and you humans can pat yourselves on the back for being the only ones in the universe to have thought of it.

I shouldn't need to say that at 600 mph everything feels really hard when it hits, but fortunately, the potato only grazed my head, but then, unfortunately, it was sucked into my jet pack. As the jet pack began sputtering and coughing, I tried to look on the bright side. The situation being what it was, any change would be an improvement, and I always liked to see a computer get a beating. The potato got me out of doing circles, and soon I was flying around, jerking right and left giving my tail whiplash until I crashed painfully into a large piece of wood. Humans call them billboards. I was invisible the whole time, but if I hadn't been the humans below would've seen an otter flying recklessly through the air with a jetpack on its back before crashing into and through an advertisement for something called the United States Air Force.

Shortly after impact the automatic safety for the jet triggered and a parachute shot out to kill the speed. Once the speed was killed, the jet pack decided to detach itself from me. I don't know why, and some day I will, and when I find the otter responsible I will exact revenge.

I landed with a lot of pain in a puddle of mud. The jetpack drifted down calmly but still landed on me with enough force that it added to the pain and made me see stars. Struggling out of the jetpack's parachute, I looked down at the mud covering my fur and wondered, "Whose fault is this?" Turning to the dented jetpack I accused, "This is your dirty doing, isn't it?"

When no response came from the jetpack or its computer, I wiped off the largest clumps of mud and muttered, "There has to be someone I can blame for this. Somebody has to pay, and it has to hurt," I insisted, throwing a clump of mud at the jetpack, "at least as much as that just did, but with interest," I added, "to compensate me for the delay in gratification."

Still getting no response from the jetpack, I looked up to the sky and thought unkind things about our Head of Pilots Derbaron, who was the otter I trusted least with my personal safety, which was true for pretty much the entire crew.

The only exceptions were the other pilots and the Man, who was of course ultimately responsible for my suffering and the obviously choice for my revenge fantasies. Unfortunately, it was inconceivable that I would get any revenge against the Man anytime soon because he was the final authority on the Determined Goat 4 and we were only 5 years into our 35-year mission. Any revenge would have to wait 30 years, and that was almost 30 years too distant in the future for my short attention span, making any revenge fantasy too unbelievable.

I needed someone or something else to blame, and since the only candidate near enough to hit was the jetpack, I decided for the moment to blame its computer.

With my mind settled, I pointed at the jetpack and hissed, "This is all your fault, you math loving piece of junk. I know it was you, and I don't care if I have to chew every piece of you apart with my bare teeth I'm going to fragment you into bits and scatter them in the ugliest place I can find."

SURVIVAL GUIDE

Welcome to the Otternot Earth Survival Guide, your one stop reference for the solutions to all earthly problems.*

* Confirmed 51% Factual Accuracy Rating

As I stepped toward the jetpack a panel on its side opened and revealed a survival kit. Seeing it, I remembered there were usually precautions in place in all Otternot operations for when accidents happened because they often did. Had I paid better attention to the orientation classes I would have known that every jetpack comes with a survival kit stocked with helpful survival gadgets.

I removed the survival kit from the jetpack and began rummaging through its items, which were disguised as rocks until held by an otter's hand. I discovered a scent detector, then a communicator, sonic amplifier, an ELF or Earth Location Finder, neural destabilizer, a PHESA or Personal Hand-held Electric Shock Administrator, rope, rations, a fire extinguisher, and then best of all, a fully charged matter destabilizer.

With the matter destabilizer in my hand, I looked over my shoulder at the jetpack with destructive thoughts going loudly through my mind. I was moving the matter destabilizer to aim it at the jetpack when it occurred to me that vaporizing the jetpack might be a bad idea. I didn't have a reason for thinking that was the case but I really wanted to do it and I had felt the same way in the past before doing things that I shouldn't have done. Based on my experience the signs were good that the idea was bad, or otherwise said, was too good to be true.

Remembering that I was basically marooned on an alien planet ruled by giant monkeys, I decided not to tempt fate by making things worse. I decided to play it safe and read the instructions in the OESG or Otternot Earth Survival Guide, a reference for Earth trivia with tips for associating with humans and instructions for dealing with most emergencies. Finding the OESG rock I navigated through its holographic display to the instructions for dealing with a crashed jetpack.

Reading the instructions I could barely believe them. The standard procedure was to trigger the jetpack's self-destruct mechanism to make it blow itself up.

I sprang into action, putting on the survival kit and following the instructions to activate the self-destruct. A timer started at 30 seconds, and I began running for cover, laughing as the seconds ticked down toward the moment of my revenge.

TIMER SET

OESG (Otternot Earth Survival Guide)

Note on Jetpack Self Destruct: After removing the survival pack from the jetpack, find the self-destruct panel and press the two black buttons at the same time. A timer will start at 30 seconds, and you should be running for cover.

I laughed all the way to the woods, where I grew silent and focused on running away faster. Moving through the Earth trees I began to wonder if my rough flight and landing were genuinely the jetpack computer's fault.

I hoped it was true so that the destruction would be a classic case of revenge and the best case scenerio, where I got to murder a computer with a large explosion.

It occurred to me that I was going to be the envy of every otter when I told the story back on the ship. I imagined the looks on their faces, and then I felt another one of my familiar feelings, one that usually meant I had just fallen into the trap of believing I was smarter or luckier than I really was, which in the past had often gotten me into serious trouble, mostly because it was only natural to want to see a smarty otter fail so it was almost impossible to resist sabataging myself once I caught myself thinking I was sure to win.

So I began to worry it had been too easy. It wasn't like a computer to die without a fight, which was half the reason it was so pleasing to finally divide one of them by zero.

Then I started to get winded from running and found a nice spot to stop and take cover. After a few seconds I wondered how many of the 30 had gone by, and then I wondered why I was winded after running less than thirty seconds. Even with the added weight of the survival kit on my back and tail I should have been able to run longer than that, and the longer I thought about it without an explosion interrupting, the more certain I became that I had been running for way longer than 30 seconds, and more importantly the self-destruct had failed.

Almost but not entirely certain I picked my communicator out of the survival kit and shouted, "Some ott help me out here! Derbaron, you got to be listening to this! I need help, you hear me? That means I need you to stop being crazy for two seconds and do something to save my life! You hear me?"

Getting no reply I consulted the OESG emergency instruction and found a short note on communication failure:

If you get no reply when speaking into your communicator the most likely issue is that the pilots of any nearby shuttles are listening to music too loudly to hear you. It's also possible those pilots don't like you or to avoid work they are all waiting for some other pilot to answer you.

"Or," I added my own update to the OESG note, "the pilot is Derbaron, and he's too busy scaring otters to death to-," and then I went quiet, noticing the communicator was still active in my hand. Putting the communicator away I suddenly grew wary, sensing deep down something was very wrong.

I looked around the alien woods for signs of danger, and then looked up through the leaves and branches at the clear blue sky. I knew Derbaron was up there somewhere, and my instincts told me he wasn't answering because he was doing something else; something that didn't include helping me.

Guessing I would regret it, I scampered back through the woods to the clearing and then crept to the jetpack. Then I saw its self-destruct was at 27 seconds. Relaxing, I pressed the two buttons to activate its self-destruct again. Nothing happened, so I pressed the buttons harder, again and again until I gave up and decided to destroy it by claw. I started by kicking it, and that was as far as I got.

As my foot connected with the jetpack self-destruct panel the timer resumed counting down but in 9 seconds increments, which meant I only had 3 real-time seconds to react, or 2 after I noticed the counter drop from 27 to 18.

In two seconds I managed to jump away from the jetpack and then the blast knocked me unconscious. I woke up hours later at the bottom of a crater with a monstrous headache but otherwise in good health despite the massive nearby explosion, thanks to the survival kit's sturdy construction and its ESCM or Emergency Survival Counter-Measure, which had expended its one-time-use charge to redirect most of the blast's force away from my also resilient body.

Finding the explosion evaporated all the mud off my fur and the survival kit slightly singed but otherwise intact, I blinked at the devastation surrounding me, and then closed my eyes to try to remember where I was and why I was there.

Slowly my headache faded and I started remembering things like my name and what I did for a living, and then the pain in my head was replaced by a growing anger.

I wasn't sure why I was angry but I was certain I was going to angrier once I figured out why. The anger continued to build while I continued to recall the recent string of tragic events I had been subjected to since the Man gave me the mission to recover Romeo, who I realized was ultimately to blame for my general misfortune, but not specifically for the recent explosion, which I assumed was the spark for my new anger.

I had always been aggravated by life-threatening accidents, probably because my mother didn't let me take enough risks as an otterling so I never got the hang of it, so I was likely mad about getting blown up, but I also felt like I was missing something I needed to know in order to get properly angry.

Then it dawned on me that I hadn't been able to enjoy the jetpack computer's demise. That joy had been stolen from me, and I knew that Derbaron was the thief because I recognized his trademarks. It was classic Derbaron, so much we had a word for it. Not for the first time, I had been Derbaroned.

Convinced my troubles were Derbaron's fault, I dealt with the situation with all the courage I could muster.

Accomplice

It was nearly dusk when I finished swearing. I then decided that the best course of action was to proceed with the mission as planned, and in order to do that, I needed to find a way to the Como Zoo. After reading the section of human means of travel in the OESG I proceeded to a highway and followed it to a wayside rest. There I placed myself on the top of a human-made structure in order to better see the noisy land transportation vehicles that the humans call cars.

I sat there watching the skies while I waited for a ride and imagined my buddy Loki from Natural Phenomenon Propagation was somewhere making crop circles and Nester from Mythological Creature Propagation was arranging another Loch Ness Monster sighting. I smiled when I thought of crazy Nero hard at work teaching his birds to drop their feces on German made automobiles, and could almost smell the laboratory stench when I thought of Pastor testing his new strains of bacteria in his eternal quest to make them immune to penicillin.

I missed the ship and the crew, and even the Man. Seeing how far out of hand things had gotten, I found myself wishing Ed had left Bill's stupid computer alone.

Eventually, I heard a steady engine noise and I looked to see a gray two-door automobile come to a stop in front of the building. A tall skinny young human male exited the vehicle and entered the building below me.

Using my NVOB's or Night Vision Otter Binoculars, I investigated the car. On the passenger seat I saw magazines, and flipping through the survival manual I found the titles. Sierra Club, Audubon and National Geographic were listed under reading materials likely to denote a human sensitive to animals. I investigated the car further and noticed small advertisements on the sides of the vehicle. One read, "Save the Whales," and another was a triangle of arrows with the word "Recycle." These were also listed in the survival manual. Another check and I saw an advertisement that said 'NRA Sucks' and I was sure I had found a friendly human.

There was another symbol I couldn't find in the survival manual, and it read, "Earth First, we'll log the other planets later." I found the first two words under animal-friendly organizations, but the rest of the statement confused me.

I didn't like being confused so I forgot about it and descended from the roof of the building structure and placed myself in the automobile, awaiting the arrival of my new human companion. I glanced back at the survival manual's recommended method of approach one more time as the human came back to the car.

The human opened the door, sat down, and looked at me. He blinked several times and then his short blond hair swayed as he turned his head to look into the backseat and then out the various windows. His blue eyes looked at me again and his mouth opened to ask, "What is this? Candid Camera?"

I waited for him to say something else but he only laughed.

Impatient to get underway. I told him, "Hello human. I'm a poor woodland creature and I've fallen victim to toxic waste. This accident has given me the capability of speech but it really hurt, and I'm still in great pain. I need your help to get to the Como Zoo to seek treatment for my injuries."

The human looked at me and then opened his mouth. "So you're like a mutant beaver, huh?"

"Mutant beaver?" I nearly disintegrated him with my matter destabilizer. "I'm an otter. What're you? Blind?"

The human nodded and looked at me closer. I opened my mouth to show him I didn't have beaver buckteeth. "Oh," he said smiling, "How come you have a backpack?"

I hadn't anticipated him noticing my survival kit. "I don't have a backpack," I informed him, switching on the survival kit's cloaking device.

"Hey, it disappeared."

"No, there never was a backpack. You're delusional, possibly from the same toxic waste."

The human laughed. "I'm talking to an otter, or an otter is talking to me. Yeah, I'd say I'm delusional, but you had a backpack. You pressed a button and it disappeared."

"No I didn't."

"Yes, you did."

"No, I didn't."

"Yes, you did."

I sighed, frustrated with the situation because the human was proving to be skilled in argumentation. I tried to think of another way to go at the problem but gave up. "No, I didn't."

"Yes, you did."

"No, I didn't."

"Yes, you did."

"No, I didn't."

"Yes, you did. Is it just invisible?" The human tried to touch the survival kit.

I snapped my teeth to shoo away his hand. "Never mind the backpack, this isn't helping. I need to get to the Como Zoo to seek treatment."

The human smiled, "You're not gonna pee in my car or anything are you?"

"How vulgar," I gasped, quite displeased with the human's lack of cooperation. So far the manual's recommended method of approach was not working. "What's the matter with you? You're a friend of nature, duty bound to help woodland creatures inconvenienced by toxic waste."

"How you figure that?"

"Your reading material…and the stickers on your car."

The human laughed again. "My ex-girlfriend put those there, but that's crazy, that means you can read too."

Obviously, there was something wrong with this human, evident by the fact that a potential mate had abandoned him. I decided the OESG wouldn't help me with him, and I resorted to my knowledge of human psychology.

"Fine. I'm an otter from outer space, and if you don't bring me to the Como Zoo I'll vaporize you." Threatening physical harm is a well-used tool of otter psychology and I assumed it would work with a human.

The human blew air through his lips so they rippled. "Pffft. Your first story was better. You sure you're not Santa Claus?"

I opened the car door and using my matter destabilizer I vaporized the building of the wayside rest. The human looked at me with less of a smile than before. "Okay. Either I'm asleep and dreaming or this is real. Oh well. Como Zoo you said?"

"Yes."

"Okay, I'm heading that way anyway. My name's Percivel Tyse. What's yours?"

"Spock." The human laughed again.

History and Customs

An hour later we were approaching a center of human population known as the Twin Cities, which weren't even close to identical. My study of the human was going very well. In ten minutes I discovered the secret of the human's game of golf, which it turned out was a waste of time, and also discovered that the human Internet was capable of other feats besides distributing images of otters. Once we'd found the otter pictures we didn't really try to find anything else, but from what Percivel or Vel told me, just about anything there was to learn about humans could be found on the Internet.

I'm sure Ed would have discovered that eventually if his wife hadn't broken the human laptop computer over his head, and in general, I was pleased with that information but our interplanetary dialogue became strained over the point of otter-human relations. "So Kirk," Percivel asked me, "you serious about humans being able to live forever?"

"My name is Spock, and yes. If you quit burning fossil fuels and maintained a diet of chocolate, strawberries, eucalyptus leaves, and ostrich feathers you'd never die, I mean, not of natural causes anyway."

"Interesting. Could you otters give us the technology so we wouldn't have to burn fossil fuels?"

"Of course, but that would be counterproductive."

The human frowned. "Counterproductive to what?"

"Well we're just waiting for you humans to die off and the Earth otters to evolve to our level," I explained patiently, "so making you live longer would slow things down."

The human's hairless face frowned deeper. "That sucks."

RIDE SHARE

OESG Note on Traffic: Traffic is a general term for rituals featuring land transport vechicles. The best known examples are the slow moving parades that occur twice daily inside major human cities known as jams. Experts debate the cultural significance of such displays.

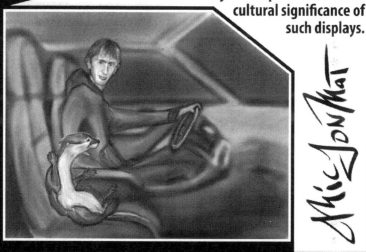

"No use helping inferior life forms to evolve."

"I guess not," he grumbled, "So we're inferior, huh?"

"Yes. In our space exploration, we have found five planets with intelligent life. All of them have had otters."

"No way. You've never found a planet without otters?"

"Oh there's Nawiat, but there's no intelligent life on it, only beavers. Earth didn't have any when we first reached it either."

The human wondered, "When was that?"

"Back when dinosaurs were here. Pretty sad times. It called for drastic measures." I explained to Percivel that we helped nature along a little bit. Back then the Earth's axis wasn't titled so there were no seasons. Tilting that axis is in our record books as possibly our greatest accomplishment. When I'm bored I sometimes watch the video of the expressions on the dinosaur's faces when the first snowflakes started falling.

But that didn't quite do the trick and not all the dinosaurs died. Then we tried breaking up the one land mass into many, and that was working but it was slow, so we altered a comet so it smacked into the Earth. Finishing the explanation I chuckled, "Nothing like a comet to shake up an ecosystem."

"So why haven't you gotten rid of us humans?"

"By the time we came back humans and otters were here at the same time, so comets were out."

"Came back? You just took off after you smoked the dinosaurs?"

"Evolution's pretty slow, slower than your human game of baseball. We weren't going to stick around and watch fish flopping around trying to walk on land. We had better things to do with the war going on."

"A war? With who?"

"Nawiat."

"The beaver planet? But you said they weren't intelligent?"

"They're not," I assured him, "They're beavers."

"Oh, well what was their problem?"

"You know beavers. They'd been building these stupid dams for thousands of years and we... well... okay so we broke a few, so what? If they didn't like building dams why'd they build them in the first place? What, do they only like doing it the one time? Does it lose the thrill after that? We see they like something and give them more practice, so how is that bad? Answer me that!"

"Oh, I can't. I entirely agree with you."

"Well, the beavers didn't. They got all touchy about it and so we had a war."

"How long did it last?"

"Oh, we finished it about five thousand years ago."

"But the dinosaurs died out what, like 65 million years back, right?"

"Something like that. Math was never my thing."

The human sounded as if he didn't believe me. "So you fought the beavers for 65 million years?"

I twitched my tail. "It was a good fight."

"Who won?"

"It was a half victory," I explained. "They agreed to build our machinery, and we promised never to set foot on their stupid planet again."

"So wait, all your stuff is built by beavers?"

"Not all of it, just the cheap junk."

"Does it work?"

"Usually. Well, half the time I guess. We try not to rely on anything with 'made in Nawiat' on it."

The human sat and thought things through for a moment. At this point, I should mention that in my survival kit there was a portable neural destabilizer, so I wasn't worried about this information being spread among the humans, and most of it was lies anyway.

Finally, he started talking again. "You know what? You guys suck. I don't even feel like helping you anymore, Mr. Superior life form. Mr. Spock."

"Truth is painful. Quit asking questions, or, as you say, deal with it."

"Deal with it? You're full of it. Superior life form? You hosers couldn't even beat the beavers in a war."

"Hey-," I began to object.

"Plus," he interrupted my objection, "beavers and otters are in the same family of species. You're related, like cousins."

"All right, human. Now you went and did it." Vel had resorted to otter bashing. I pulled off the gloves. "Listen to this. I'll tell you all about the humans."

"Now I like to think we've been fair with you humans over the years, but you didn't make things easy. Oh, we tried to be nice at first, teaching you how to build and fish and grow crops and make beavers into hats, but time after time all we got back was ingratitude."

"Take those rotten Atlanteans. We gave them lots of technology and taught them how to put it to use. We even helped build their city on that island. We thought it was good fun, a nice experiment, but what happened to Atlantis? Those ingrates had the gall to build idols to worship and we otters pretend to like freedom of religion as much as anyone, but we don't take insults lightly. I mean, one day they tell us they've patterned a God after us, and we thought they'd achieved a small bit of wisdom for two minutes and then they take the cover off the thing and I've seen the pictures and it was no otter; it was clearly a dirty dam building beaver."

"And we didn't hold a grudge. After we blew Atlantis up we tried again with the Egyptians and helped them build the pyramids. What'd they do? They did the same thing. They made a whole batch of gods, like way more than ten, and they didn't make one an otter. Of course they said we hadn't bothered to look at them all, and we'd stopped after the first ten so we let that slide, but then their king died and those mummy makers tried to stuff our ambassador and that's how much we put up with before we got the message and quit trying to help you monkeys."

The human glanced away from the road to me to ask, "That's how much it took?"

"We're willing to say patience is a good thing, so we are capable of it."

"Yeah, that's some pretty epic patience, but so what have you been doing since then? Just watching us... monkeys?"

"No. First, we smashed the nose off that stupid human-headed lion the Egyptians had."

"And then?"

"Then we taught the Egyptians how to tax the peasants."

"And after that?"

"After that, we started introducing species to pester you hairless monkeys, like mosquitoes and goats and dragons and sea monsters," I waved my paw in the air to pick out one more of the many, "skunks."

The human laughed again. "Well, that hasn't worked."

"No, your sun made the dragons go blind and they kept crashing into mountains, and did you know you have really big things with tentacles in your oceans?"

"Yeah, giant squids."

"That's them. Jerks. They ate all our sea monsters, and then we got a bunch more regulations and couldn't introduce species after that so we looked into microscopic organisms."

"So you've been trying to kill us with biological warfare?"

I was startled at the thought. "No, that would be going too far. We were just trying to make a bacteria or virus that'll make all you humans grow tails and turn you into otters."

"Well, I know that hasn't worked."

"Something always goes wrong. The Black Plague, Smallpox, Influenza, Syphilis, but we'll get it right one day."

"Yeah, well, like I said, your first story about the nuclear waste was better, Kirk."

"My name is Spock, quit calling me Kirk." I decided to ask the human, "Besides, what do you know? Not much. I could put everything you know on the tip of my tail."

"Maybe you should haul your tail on foot, you ingrate," the human said with audible contempt, "Carjacking weasel."

"Weasel?" That was almost as bad as a beaver. During the war with the beavers, we genetically engineered weasels to fight for us. That was at the end, and it was actually the way we defeated the beavers. It didn't go as planned, of course, since the weasels were too stupid to follow orders and didn't like the water, so instead of fighting the beavers they went and chased the squirrels and rabbits, which all started gathering around the beavers for protection, and since the beavers didn't like the rabbits and squirrels they had to sue for peace.

"Weasel?" I repeated.

"Weasel, beaver, otter, muskrat, same thing."

"Muskrat?" Muskrats are basically stupid beavers. That was the last straw. "Stop the car!" I ordered.

"No."

"Stop the car or I'll open the door!"

The human shrugged and said, "Go ahead."

I gripped the handle. "I'll do it!"

"I said go ahead," Vel said, pressing a button on his own door. Something on my door moved, and I heard a click. "Go for it," the human encouraged me, "Make my day, rodent."

Pushing hard against the door I forced it open. I was acting under the impression the human car worked like one of our shuttles, which as a safety precaution are rigged so that when a door is opened they automatically slow down and land. I'd read somewhere that human trains were equipped with brake cords mounted over the passenger seats that could be pulled by anyone in case of an emergency. It was this concept we modeled our shuttles after, and of course, for the first month otters were opening doors just for fun, but that didn't matter because at that moment I was assuming the human car would stop automatically when I opened the door.

When the car stopped I intended to either use the neural destabilizer to wash Vel's memory, or if I was still mad, to vaporize him with my matter destabilizer, but what happened, of course, was the car didn't stop and I was sucked outside it.

Transport Safety

We otters have extensively genetically engineered bodies to help us cheat death and physics to survive the accidents we encounter by chance or that occur because we guessed wrong.

In the case of the car, which was traveling 75 mph over a surface horizontally, when I left the car I was also traveling at 75 mph horizontally, but without the car's thrust gravity quickly lowered my altitude, and the result is best defined as a 'skipping' situation, which was an alternating mix of being in contact with the ground and being airborne. I was going to basically skip along the roadway until my speed slowed me into a 'skidding' situation which I'd be in until I stopped.

*B*LOWFISH *M*ANEUVER

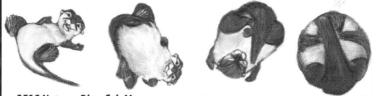

OESG Note on Blowfish Maneuver: Earth's environment is conducive to all Otternot body alterations including every otter's best friend the blowfish maneuver, which can save you from most of the common dangers found on Earth. For a reminder on performing safe blowfish maneuver, please consult your mother, just in case she's been wanting to talk to you.

Getting dropped from the jetpack was different. That was a 'splatting' situation, which is a specific form of the more general 'bouncing' situation, and my momentum was stopped nearly instantaneously by splatting on the ground, or the mud puddle, and in turn the jetpack experienced a more typical bouncing situation when it landed on me and then bounced off my body and into the mud, although some might call that a 'skipping' situation because of the angle of the bounce.

That's an important difference because with bouncing there isn't much you can do, you only have one impact to deal with so you just splat against something hopefully soft, but with skipping you have a few options, so knowing that I was going to start skipping I sucked in as much air as I could and curled up into a ball. This trick is called a blowfish maneuver, or going into blowfish configuration.

In blowfish configuration, I was able to roll peacefully along the road, using my fur as a natural absorbent to come out of the potentially fatal experience without even what the humans call carpet burn. That's what would've happened, but I was wearing the survival kit on my back, and therefore my blowfish configuration was flawed. The sphere of my body had a bulge, and this caused me to bounce-skid, a combination of the two situations discussed above.

It went like this: rolling, survival kit hits the ground, launching into the air, landing, pain, slight bouncing, more slight bouncing, rolling again, survival kit hits the ground, launching into the air, and so on. This repeated itself until during one of the bouncing phases when my bouncing cast me off the road and against a nearby tree, which was a purely bouncing situation because the tree completely stopped my momentum. The impact also knocked me unconscious.

I awoke to something coarse rubbing over my face and decided that I hadn't been dreaming, that I actually was rolling down a human roadway, and so I immediately executed a blowfish maneuver and puffed up. Of course, as I learned shortly after, I wasn't moving. It was light out, and therefore morning, and in the faint light, I could see a wolf with its tongue wagging, the tongue that had been licking my face.

Over Friendly

OESG Note on Wildlife:

The local earth wildlife is typically shy, often playing at not wanting to play, but with effort some can be convinced to interact and others go out of their way to engage, which often are the ones that enjoy fighting.

See: prey, predators

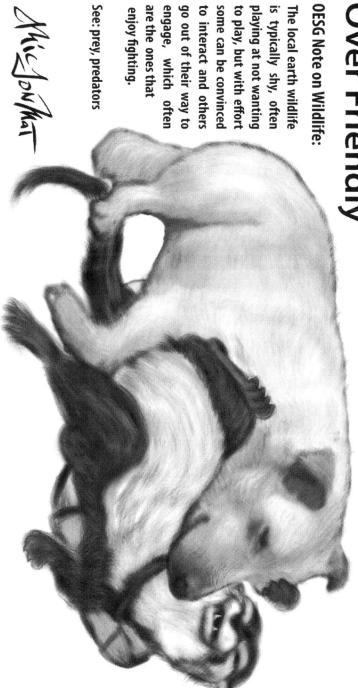

I sighed in relief and spoke to the wolf in its native tongue, which sounds to humans like barking. It isn't; the intonations are just too subtle for human ears to detect. Despite having superior ears the wolf didn't seem to understand, judging from the expression on its face, which was thoroughly vacant.

The wolf looked at me stupidly, and then walked up and licked my face again. "Stop," I told it. "Cease!" It kept licking me. "Desist! Halt!" It kept licking me. "Yield!" At the last command, the wolf backed away and closed its mouth. I was confused. The wolves didn't speak human as far as I knew.

I tried another command. "Sit?"

The wolf sat on its hind legs.

"Lay down."

The wolf laid down.

"Aha!" I said, realizing I'd been deceived. I had assumed the wolf before me, which the more I thought about it didn't even look like a wolf, was a member of the Pack.

I'd been lying to the human earlier concerning intelligent life in the universe. There's actually quite a bit of it besides us otters, but the other life forms don't bother with the human planet. They're all happy where they are and think space travel is for the birds, or at least for the otters.

We're about the only adventurous ones out there, besides the wolves, who like to travel in space and find planets, but they don't bother with Earth because humans live there.

The wolves like to find uninhabited planets they develop and populate, and I suppose that's not a bad thing. It seems a little tedious to us otters, but we don't say that out loud because wolves get grumpy when you lip off to them, and they're a lot bigger than us.

What I said about the weasels solving the Beaver War wasn't true either. The wolves were just sick of the fighting and told us otters to quit bothering the beavers or they'd cause our sun to go nova. Now when I saw the Earth wolf, I assumed a Pack ship had gone off course and landed on Earth and had, coincidentally, come to my rescue, but that wasn't the case.

Because the Earth wolf was responding to my human verbal commands, I realized one of our conspiracy theories was, in fact, true. We knew there were wolves on Earth, but we never told the Pack about it. We also kept the fact that dolphins were in the oceans secret from the Space Dolphins. We kept a lot of secrets actually, and it was necessary because whenever it gets out that we're screwing with an inhabited planet everybody else gets upset about it and makes us quit.

So we knew there were primitive wolves on Earth, and it was popular rumor that the humans had put the wolves to work. The ruling otters back on Revir were so worried it would get out that they kept it secret from even their own subjects because they knew one of us would sell that information to the wolves. See the rulers on Revir have interests to protect. Earth supplies some of our best TV shows, it's a veritable ocean of entertainment, and if it gets out the rotten humans are being mean to wolves the Pack will come down and wipe out all our fun.

Now I knew it was true. The humans had enslaved the wolves, and I was looking at one such slave. So subordinated was the poor thing that it responded to verbal commands. I felt sorry for it, momentarily.

Then I sensed an idea forming. A few moments later the idea finished forming, and then I named the Earth wolf Gomer. Then I decided to use it as a means of transportation.

By filling up certain bones with air I reshaped my body to be able to ride on Gomer's back, as otterlings like to do with adult otters. This arrangement didn't seem to disturb Gomer, as I expected. Having been subjected to human enslavement, I assumed he had no real will of his own.

I checked my positioning device and established in what exact direction to proceed. Unfortunately, that was the direction of the human road, and neither Gomer nor I liked that idea, so I pointed my mount in the less exact direction of basically south, and kicked with my heels.

Gomer responded with a burst of speed in the direction of south into a group of trees. At this point, I ducked and closed my eyes. I heard branches snapping and felt leaves brushing my fur. While Gomer continued to bound over fallen trees and rocks I could also feel his back muscles flex, but mostly I felt shock after horrible shock to my otter jewels.

This continued for some time as the beast tore through the underbrush, and it only ended, as I discovered upon regaining consciousness for a second time, because Gomer had noticed a dead bird along the path. Noticing the bird Gomer stopped dead and sent me flying from his back into another bouncing situation with another tree.

Awakened once more by Gomer's tongue I ate three emergency pain pills from my allegedly indestructible survival kit. While everything inside was intact at that point, the protective covering was beginning to dent and tear.

My head hurt too badly to think about it just then. Eating the pills I shooed Gomer away and thought about how to handle the problem of riding the Earth wolf. After thinking about it, and climbing a tree to get away from Gomer so I could think about it without being interrupted, I was then forced to throw him some emergency food from my survival kit because he wouldn't stop barking at me. Gomer didn't think much of the food so I set my neural destabilizer to its highest setting and shot a bird. On that high a level a neutral destabilizer fries the brains of small animals, and so the bird died and Gomer shut up and ate it.

I decided a simple rope would be the proper method for securing my body. Gomer already had a collar of some sort, so I took a simple rope from inside the survival kit and tied it first to his collar, and then around myself underneath my arms.

I remounted Gomer, pointed him in the right direction and kicked my heels. The burst of speed came once again, the trees snapped, the leaves went by, everything the same as before. For about five minutes I was thinking I'd solved my problem, but then Gomer happened upon a rabbit.

Rabbits are tricky little vermin to be sure, and Gomer shared my distaste for them. He chased the big-eared rodent as best he could, but it was clear to me the rabbit was playing games. It was going through some of the smallest openings and into the unkindest thorny bushes.

In one of the small openings, Gomer was forced to crawl on his belly. Seeing it coming I abandoned ship you might say.

Thinking I'd saved myself I began pulling out some of the thorns while Gomer reached the other side of the small passage and resumed running again at full speed.

I was picking a thorn from my tail when my mind finally remembered that the rope tied to me was also tied to Gomer, and then I felt a tightening an instant before I was jerked through the small opening and thereafter dragged wherever Gomer felt like going for the next five minutes.

Following the rabbit, who I was beginning to really hate, Gomer went over rocks, down steep hills, through bushes, and around trees. Without much choice in the matter, I tried at first to get the rope off my body but then decided to perform the blowfish maneuver and save myself. Of course, I still had the survival kit attached to my back, so the same roll-roll-bump-crash-bounce-crash-bounce-crash-roll took place.

Our journey ended when Gomer decided to jump in a lake. Not being an expert on stupid human enslaved Earth wolves I can't tell you why that made sense to Gomer. I didn't really care at the time. I just trashed around freeing myself of the rope and struggled to dry land while Gomer paddled around the lake in some perverted form of swimming.

Sitting on the shore I thought of new ways to fasten myself to Gomer, but I quickly noticed the water had caused Gomer to stink worse than something dead for a week so I gave up. Gomer went splashing in the lake again and as I watched him, I noticed strange things floating in the water. I'm not sure what they were, but they weren't just floating, they were moving. I took a closer look at the lake and decided it wasn't a lake, but a river. Not just a river; it was flowing south.

Being an otter, I knew what to do.

Otter Natural

Solo Traveling

My experiences with Gomer had made me suspicious of anything human made or trained. In that mindset I swam alone down the river, hoping it would flow right by the Como Zoo.

Now my positioning device had the most accurate maps possible of the area, and I could've checked them to see exactly where the river went, but I didn't. I didn't because I knew if I looked I'd be disappointed, and for the length of the river trip I wanted to cling to hope. I only made it two miles down river thanks to the clumsy survival kit and being bashed around by Gomer. My tail was sprained so I could barely use it, and the rest of my muscles were bruised and sore. Blowfish maneuver or not, bouncing situation or skidding situation, I had gotten the fur beat off me, and I needed to rest.

I took that rest on the opposite side of the river from Gomer, who was following me downstream and barking to let me know he could still see me. I don't know whose idea it was, but the survival kit had been made to float so I couldn't submerge beneath the water's surface and get away from Gomer. So Gomer and I, sitting on opposite sides of the river, watched one another. I was eating survival ration 748, which tastes somewhere between brook trout and loon. It's not too bad. Gomer was barking at me and occasionally biting his tail while doing some strange circling dance.

It reminded me of the loop monkey, what we call our most advanced primate on Revir.

Since humans were discovered there's been a debate about whether or not we should exterminate all the loop monkeys since they might evolve into humans sometime in the future. I'm not for one side of the debate or the other, I mean, I don't hate loop monkeys; I think everyone should own one.

That's what we've been doing with them since they were discovered. Loop monkeys, or loopeys, are as fun to watch as two badgers tied together by the tail. Just give the loopeys an Iky tree to play in and they're fine and fun and do their weird little dances.

Old Windar, the head of Primate Evolutionary Studies on

the ship, once told me his theory on the loopeys and the Iky trees.

"Put that skull down and listen up Spock. Now, we've found Iky trees everywhere right?"

"No," I disagreed, "there aren't any on Earth."

"Yeah, that's what I said."

I disagreed again. "No, you didn't."

"Yes, I did."

"No, you didn't."

"Yes, I did!"

I settled in for some intense debating over the matter. "I suppose that it's possible that you... didn't!."

"Okay fine, I said it poorly but that's what I meant. Earth is the only planet without Iky trees, and it's the only planet with humans. You know where humans come from right?"

"Of course," I lied. "Where?"

"Monkeys, well kinda, something like that, same family anyway and basically just mice in the end, but listen. You know what's special about the Iky trees?"

"They stink about as bad as the Man."

"Sure, but besides that the nuts produced by the Iky tree, you know how they work?"

"No," I told him, "nuts were never my thing."

"Well, right, see you have this nut, and it's really hard. Squirrels can't even chew through it, nothing can, and so nothing eats them; except for the loopeys."

"How?"

"Their fancy thumbs. With their thumbs, the loopeys can get inside the nuts and eat the stuff inside. Because of the way the nuts are designed, the primates are the only ones that can get inside at the good stuff." Windar started smiling happily. I assumed he'd taught me something profound, but I hadn't understood anything.

"What do you mean the stuff inside the nuts?"

"I mean the stuff inside the nuts."

I nodded, "Yeah, and isn't there a word for it besides the stuff inside the nuts, and never mind, I don't care. Anyway, I get you, the monkeys can eat the nuts, and beavers are dumb.

Big deal. So what? What's my motivation for caring?"

"Because it's interesting," Windar insisted, "Do you know why loopeys are always doing those crazy dances?"

I thought about it intensely for an instant, and then gave it my best guess, "They're cross-eyed? That's it, isn't it?"

"No you slobbering fool, the Iky tree's nuts are poisonous, but it's like no other poison. See all types of plants try to defend themselves, right? They have hard nut shells, or they're poisonous or the seeds are thorny or they just don't taste good. They're trying to survive, but see, the Iky tree does it a different way. Its poison works at two levels. On the first level, it tastes really good and makes you happy, like a drug. Oh yeah, don't tell anybody about this by the way."

"I won't," I lied.

"Yeah, so it's a happy drug, and that's why the monkeys do those dances, cause they're in the state we call AMCU, or All Monkey Crazied Up, but then on another level the Iky tree poison alters DNA throughout the body of anything that eats it and destroys any unstable DNA."

"Does that kill the monkeys?"

"No, but think about mutations and evolution. By eating the Iky tree poison the loopeys never get a chance to evolve because any unstable DNA, like a mutation, gets burned off so they just stay the same. They quit evolving."

"Okay," I said. "So what?"

"Well, because Iky trees are on every single planet except for Earth, the Iky tree nuts have stopped the primates from evolving beyond loop monkeys. It's a funny little paradox. They've become so adapted that they're the only creature that can get into certain goodies, so they're the most successful organism in that regard, and yet those goodies end up turning them into simpletons, or preventing them from evolving into something greater. Neat, huh?"

"So what about humans?"

"Because there aren't any Iky trees on Earth," Windar explained, "the primates were able to continue evolving into that greater thing, which is a human."

"So," I wondered, "if we planted a ton of Iky trees on Earth would all these human super monkeys stop evolving?"

Windar nodded. "If they ate the Iky tree nuts."

"Hmm," I hummed, considering the possibilities.

Then Windar added, "It's also a cure for cancer."

That was a possibility that hadn't occurred to me. "Oh, that figures, you know? Well, that's out then," I said with a shrug.

"Yeah," Windar nodded happily before frowning and then ordering me, "Put that skull down."

After that I think Windar and I sneaked into the ship's air vents so we could get to the panel in Ed's office and throw things at him while he was trying to work, or something like that but back on the Earth's surface, at the river's edge, having rested and recollected, I went back into the water and tried to swim. Gomer kept following along the riverbank and barking until I got tired of trying to swim, then I inflated my body so it floated and tied the rope I'd been using to ride Gomer onto my survival kit and let it float behind me while letting the river carry me along wherever the river happened to be going.

Still annoyed by Gomer's barking, I turned on my personal cloaking device and the survival kit's, hoping to disappear and get rid of the Earth wolf to float peacefully, but it didn't work because even a slave Earth wolf has a good sense of smell so Gomer still knew I was there. Plus cloaking devices don't work very well in the water, as Nester the Head of Mythological Creature Propagation will tell you.

Nester loves using cloaking devices to make humans see things that aren't there. His favorite, the Loch Ness Monster, is probably the best example. When the humans think they're seeing something beneath the water's surface it's really Nester on a Jet Ski with a cloaking device turned on. He claims the weirdness on the water surface excites the human imagination.

But I wasn't on a Jet Ski, so I wasn't making any waves, so what a person would've seen if they'd been looking were two dents in the water. I continued on like that for a couple hours, drifting along being a dent in the water while Gomer barked and everything else did whatever else seemed reasonable at the time according to physics, priorities and abilities.

Chapter 3

Misinformation

Hearing human automobile noises, I woke up from yet another nap and checked behind me to make sure the dimple in the water from my survival kit was still there, but instead I found there was no dimple; just the survival kit floating.

I swam to shore, which happened to be under a bridge, and checked the battery for the survival kit's cloaking device. It was empty. No more power. I checked inside the survival kit for an extra power supply, but I found that the charging unit, which operated off solar power, had been damaged.

I was beginning to worry but I didn't panic and opened the OESG. In the chapter on power supplies I noticed this entry:

All cloaking devices are equipped to use the power supplied by a human battery type 3-A. These can be obtained at the same places humans regularly fill their transport machines with fossil fuels. The common term is 'gas station' and such locations can be commonly found along lanes of transport. Alternatively, small human electronic devices use type 3-A batteries, and therefore such human electronic devices can be used of for power.

Note – if obtaining type 3-A batteries from human electronic devices carried by humans exercise caution and be sure to use a neural destabilizer. Recommended method: use neural destabilizer on medium high setting to incapacitate human initially and therefore eliminate the possibility of forgetting to do it later.

Understandably, after my dealings with Vel, I was leery of the OESG's advice. While it was possible that Vel was just a degenerate, there was also the possibility that the OESG I was depending upon for my survival contained only average otter type information.

Most otter books are that way or at least the how-to books. The main purpose of these books is to be interesting, but sometimes there is more interest for the community of otters if one otter learns an incorrect procedure for something and then blows that something up.

It's all about limits. Common sense would say that manuals for disarming bombs should be concise and truthful, and that's the way they are now after the publishers of the first Disarming Bombs for Stotters were sued and forced to revise the book. It wasn't much; they just had to rearrange the sequence for cutting the various colored wires so the procedure didn't cause the bomb to go off. A stotter, incidentally, is a stupid otter.

And otter law is very clear on the subject of physical injury to otters by otters through any means and whether it's accidental or deliberate. Otter law states its okay as long as it's not fatal, which is common sense. Even the best of us otters can't find something funny when it kills us. That's impossible.

Consider the differences between the books Identifying Plant Species for Stotters, Identifying Poisonous Mushrooms for Stotters, and Calculating Incoming Asteroids for Stotters.

Now in the first case, if something like poison ivy is identified incorrectly and an otter happens to suffer a little scratching, it's not a big deal. After the rash goes away the otter will laugh about it, and then play the same dirty trick on his friends, and therefore there are very few correct identifications of plants in Identifying Plant Species for Stotters, except for the last ¼ of the book. It was about then that the author got bored and quit screwing around.

Now, as far as the poisonous mushrooms go, there isn't as much room for humor, but there is still some because not all poisonous mushrooms are fatal. Some have interesting effects and knowing this the publisher of Identifying Poisonous Mushrooms for Stotters took certain liberties and confused certain species and so instead of getting a harmless tasty mushroom a few otters ate some that caused them to think beavers were chasing them. That's wasn't too bad, but it led to a shortage of such mushrooms, and then, given the confusion it caused, there were widespread attempts to find which other mushrooms were incorrectly identified and because of the ensuing fatalities the book was finally changed.

Of course, for Calculating Incoming Asteroids for Stotters there wasn't any room at all for mistakes as an incorrect identification could mean the death of every otter on a ship, and as there's always the off-chance that the otter that wrote the books is on that ship too, there isn't anything in that book but the facts. But those types of books, the ones with just the facts, aren't very interesting and usually aren't very long.

Calculating Incoming Asteroids for Stotters is one page and translated to human it's only 25 words.

Find an otter the computer likes and have that otter ask the computer if the asteroid is going to hit the ship, like right now.

I could go on, but the point is that how-to books such as the OESG can't be trusted to be in the best interests of the otter who is in the situation where the information is necessary.

I didn't know which category the OESG belonged. Was it completely dependable? Was it halfway serious? Was it complete beaver spit?

It seemed to me the OESG was way too long to be fully serious, but it was also too long for it to be completely serious. That's how you can tell usually. If it's really short, it's dependable. If an otter could've written it in less than a week, it's probably loaded with misinformation, and if it's long and somewhat boring, part of it will be serious and part of it won't. Usually, the stuff at the end will be the serious part.

It's sad when you realize your own species is as undependable as a Nawiat tail warmer and I was disgusted with the whole thing. Having no choice but to continue I decided the bridge above me was a transport lane and I took the OESG, left my survival kit and went up to have a look.

Batteries Included

Not far from the bridge was an oddly shaped structure that I hoped was a gas station. I took off to see, and getting close I noticed the unmistakable smell of fossil fuels.

Happy as a neutered lemming about the whole thing, I went up to the building and looked around. Taking advantage of a door opening I got inside. My personal cloaking device was still working so I wasn't noticed. I glanced at the OESG for the

61

preferred method of obtaining type 3-A batteries.

In the OESG, as with all otter books, the author responsible for each entry is identified so that if the information proves incorrect, the otter that found it to be incorrect can exact some type of vengeance, usually after getting out of the hospital, and this particular entry about obtaining type 3-A batteries was written by none other than Mikey Fish, the Head of Human Sociology.

Because I'm the Head of Human Psychology, many otters mistakenly assume that I get along with the Head of Human Sociology. In actuality, the two departments are bitter enemies, almost as bad as the Earth Security Department and the Earthling Destruction Department. Those two departments used to be together as the Earth Otter Action Oversight Committee, which formerly decided what Otternots were allowed to do on Earth. Way back before my time the two groups split because they couldn't agree on the issue of introducing a bunch of genetically engineered radioactive weasels onto Earth. One group thought it'd be a good way to solve the human problem, and the other group disagreed.

So they split and went about doing their own things but the Earth Security Department took most of the authority with it, because it has a shorter name, and so they pretty much control what can be done and the Earthling Destruction Department does whatever it can get away with and so the Earth Security Department has to try to catch them, and it's a big mess.

The conflict between Human Sociology and Psychology isn't that bad. We both agree that humans have brains, but the Sociology stotters keep trying to explain things while we psychology otts don't think it's worth the effort. The Sociology stotters also know that we Psychology otts don't really know or do anything, as most of them are the nerds that switched their majors after they found out Human Psychology was more about style and less about dressing up lab rats in pretty summer clothes, or whatever they do in Human Sociology. I know they try to get us in trouble, but that's not enough to make me actually learn anything about them.

Now, as the Head of Human Sociology, Mikey Fish was my

mortal enemy, and I didn't feel right taking any of his dirty advice. But then I decided that Mikey Fish was known for not being able to take a joke and that just about equals not being able to make a joke, so the information was probably accurate. Of course, not being able to make a good joke didn't mean he wouldn't try. That meant that if he was making a joke it was a bad one. I didn't like it one bit.

Feeling unprepared for what lay ahead, I waited until the room was empty of all humans except the man behind the counter. Jumping onto the counter, I sucked air into my ear tendons and made them look like horns and then altered the fur on my tail so it had three spikes and then turned my fur hairs so they reflected a deep red light. Then I turned off my cloaking device and waited for the human to notice me.

His eyes went big and his mouth dropped.

"Hello," I said.

"Um..." he mumbled.

"Listen here human. I am the devil. I command you to give me type 3-A batteries."

"Um..." he mumbled.

"Give me type 3-A batteries, or I will torment your soul in Hell for all eternity."

The young male human looked at me, and then slowly took a package from a rack near him. "Triple A?"

"Yes. Place them at my feet."

The human looked at me, and after looking around placed the package before me on the counter.

I said, "Thank you," and picked them up.

"Um, that'll be $4.56."

I snapped my teeth and he jumped back. "The devil," I said, "does not pay for batteries."

With that, I turned on my cloaking device and disappeared from his view. I jumped down and made my way out.

I'd been concentrating so much on the project at hand that I didn't bother to look around more carefully. Walking back to the bridge I noticed that I was at least near to a large urban development. I decided to look at my positioning device when I got back to the survival kit.

Going underneath the bridge I was greeted by Gomer, who had used the bridge to get across the river. He'd been occupying himself by chewing on the survival kit and eating most of my survival rations.

Seeing me, or rather smelling me since I still had my cloaking device on, he ran in my direction, and then not seeing me he ran me over. I don't know what the stupid Earth wolf was thinking, but he must have realized he'd hit something because he turned around and ran back, and ran over me again. This happened twice more before I turned the cloaking device off and allowed myself to be affectionately mauled.

After that pleasantry, I went about putting my survival kit back together and used the type 3-A batteries to get its cloaking device working. Then I went to check my position on the positioning device.

The positioning device is white, long and narrow. On either side are knobs for holding it. I guess it must have resembled something Gomer liked to chew on because that's what he'd taken the most interest in. It was dented and scraped, and more or less broken beyond use. I activated its self-destruction timer and threw it into the river.

Gomer ran me over again running after the positioning device. I decided it would serve him right if he got blown up and took out my Night Vision Otter Binoculars, which worked just fine in daylight. I was using them to get a better look around when I heard Gomer panting beside me, and a beep.

I turned, and there was Gomer with the positioning device in his mouth. He dropped it at my feet and ran away barking. The positioning device blew up and sent me flying through the air as I executed the blowfish maneuver.

Harnessing Power

Seeing as how I was burdened with Gomer, and I couldn't bring myself to blast him with my matter destabilizer, I decided to put the Earth wolf to use. How I intended to do this involved Gomer, the survival kit, and myself.

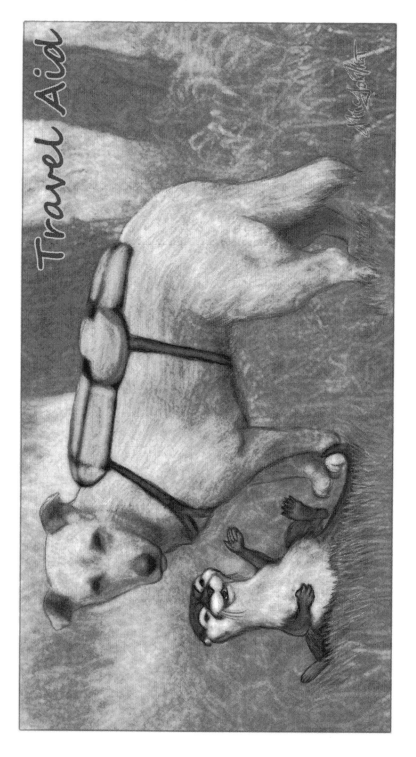

Travel Aid

So far I had learned that Gomer was prone to erratic directional shifts, accelerations and stops. He didn't seem to mind any of it, and anything loosely attached to him seemed to do the majority of the suffering. I decided that his actions did not inflict harm upon himself, and in order to prevent injury to myself, I would have to be as firmly attached as possible.

How I intended to do this was to fasten the survival kit to Gomer and then to wedge myself between the pack and him. I started by lengthening the survival kit straps, and then putting it around Gomer's body. This took the better half of an hour because Gomer felt the need to bite, maul and play with the survival kit whenever I approached him. Twice he grabbed it in his teeth and ran away and tried to bury it.

Despite these difficulties, I managed to get the rapidly deteriorating pack onto him, and then I managed to get myself wedged into position. By poking Gomer with my claws I managed to send him off in the right direction.

The same bouncing and jarring were present, but now I didn't have to worry about being thrown free or getting dragged, and I didn't have to worry about Gomer squeezing underneath a tree either as his path took us onto paved human streets. It seemed we were stopping at every tree for Gomer to mark his territory, something not completely breed out of the Earth wolves, and this did slow us down but I didn't know where we were or how to get where I was going, so I didn't mind much. I knew I needed to keep heading south and that was enough for the moment.

I let Gomer do his business and tried to go to sleep. Then I got to thinking and it occurred to me that I was using a well-known method of otter transportation, or not transportation exactly, more of a sport played with doubles where one otter was riding on the shoulders of another.

It's a good sport, not like golf. It's otter polo and it's the most popular sport worldwide on Revir. I don't like to brag, but I was pretty good at it. Our city took 13th at Regionals, and it was largely because of my abilities. Otters were talking about me going professional and I had spent many hours of my young life dreaming about being an otter polo star.

OTTER POLO

Experts debate if Otter Polo is Revir's national sport because it's also the principle cause of several kinds of injuries, or if that dynamic is nothing more than an innocent coincidence. Those same experts are split on whether the answer is worth figuring out.

Goverments across Revir fund minor Otter Polo leagues, despite the studies that show that most otters who pursue a profressional Otter Polo career never get to live out that dream and end up at least sad, and usually unskilled in a useful trade, if not handicapped.

Unfortunately while studying in college I developed a close friendship with a female otter and she made me quit, and then by the time I dropped her I was out of training, and despite a brutal training regime, I failed to make the college team.

But I still enjoy a game of otter polo now and then. It's a great sport and a great way to stay in shape. It also keeps the reflexes sharp.

The way otter polo works is that there are two teams, or four teams really because each team has one team for bearers and one for strikers. The strikers ride on the backs of the bearers, and before the match, the two groups fight to see which gets to be the striker and bearer teams.

So there are otters riding on the shoulders of other otters, and everyone is in a big pool of water. In the center of the pool is a floating ball roughly the size of a pumpkin that's almost big enough to squeeze a beaver into. Each of the strikers is armed with a big wooden mallet, but they don't use it to hit the ball, that's the bearer's job.

Whenever a bearer grabs the ball, that pair of otters is safe and can't be touched for fifteen seconds, after which the ball must be passed. Any other otter within ten feet of the ball is free game and can be hit by the strikers with the mallets. That's basically the way the game goes. The bearers throw the ball between each other and try to get it in an area where a striker from the other team isn't paying attention.

When a striker gets knocked off the bearer, both otters are out for the game and have to leave the pool. When one team is out of the pool, the other team wins.

Otter polo is great fun, and there's also a lot of strategy involved. For instance, sometimes it's better to hit the bearer underneath the striker because the bearer can't really move, and if you knock the bearer out then both him and the striker fall over. Another tactic is mallet throwing. Nothing says you can't attack a striker near the ball with a thrown mallet, and so that's what some otters do. Of course, you better make sure to get your mallet back afterward or you're a prime target.

And the strikers aren't as important as the bearers. See, the strikers get all the glory, but if the best strikers in Revir went up against a team with the best bearers in Revir, the team with the best bearers would win. It's all about positioning. Any otter can bash another otter over the head when it's an easy shot, but it takes a smart bearer to give the striker the opening, and a good bearer will recover thrown mallets, and one time as a bearer I managed to steal a mallet from a striker, so both the striker and I were attacking other players. Also, a good bearer won't let go when the striker gets knocked unconscious. He'll hold on and try to get to safety to wait for the striker to move again. The Revir championships were won that way a couple years ago.

Of course what a bearer really needs is endurance, because in important games there are always MVP's chosen and the way they get chosen is that after one team has won, that team fights among each other freestyle until just one striker bearer combo is left, and for that you need a bearer that doesn't poop out after ten minutes. You never know how long an otter polo game will last. It could take anywhere from five minutes to 2 hours, and a bearer has to keep moving the whole time or the striker's a sitting duck.

I decided that Gomer would be what we call wurer, or wussy bearer. A wurer is too scared to play well; he leans forward so the striker is sure to get bashed, and the stupid Earth wolf would have made a great wurer. He was completely at ease letting me get hit as he ran around fences and peed on trees. Fortunately, most of the blows were descending upon the survival kit, and I had my eyes closed so I couldn't anticipate the pain. As such, after an hour of running generally south, I didn't know what was going on when I heard humans yelling and Gomer yelped in surprised.

Quickly we were caught and caged.

Imprisonment

After the door shut everything went quiet, except for Gomer who didn't seem to like being caged. He was barking, scrambling around and tripping as the cage we were in began moving. I felt safe peaking out from underneath the survival kit, and not seeing anyone, I freed myself.

Inside the cage, there were vibrations that reminded me of Vel's car. Everything was metal and stored in small drawers. Nothing was lying in the open for Gomer to chew on. I assumed this vehicle was used for the purpose of abducting Earth wolves.

I complimented myself on having the cloaking devices turned on. Whoever had abducted Gomer hadn't seen me. Wondering what kinds of humans were abducting Earth wolves I looked out the window on one side of the metal cage. Outside was the human road passing away from me. It was the wrong window, so I looked out the other one.

There, seated comfortably were two humans that looked out of proportion. I think fat is the word in English, but at the time I didn't wish to be that harsh because when they'd snared Gomer he'd been running full speed and for that a good physical condition was necessary. Then I thought about it and realized I was mistaken; when Gomer was snared he was running full speed, but the snare caught him from the front and behind. Gomer must have been running toward these men. That meant they didn't need to be in good physical shape and so I could call them fat.

The two fat men were talking as they drove down the human roadway. I couldn't make out what they were speaking about since they were also playing some annoying type of music I assumed was meant to frighten the Earth wolves into obedience. Unfamiliar with the protocol the humans followed in Earth wolf abductions, I didn't know what to expect. All I had to base my expectations on was the protocol we otters use for human abductions.

Gobbels, the head of Human Abductions, whatever else he might be, still does his job well, and can be basically trusted to pull off the average abduction without killing the human and the process starts at the very beginning, the selection. The selection consists of finding some unsuspecting human alone and then shining really bright lights in the human's eyes. Then, using sophisticated electronic devices to unlock or remove any barriers, like car doors, the abducting otter than either finds a big stick or uses an otter polo mallet to bash the human on the head.

They do try to be discreet and not to kill the human, of course, but since the human's memory is going to get wiped of the whole experience, and we have sophisticated medical assistance available, it's usually not necessary to be too discreet or be too gentle with the mallet, but then all things considered an otter usually takes great care not to damage the otter polo mallet if one is being used, as a good mallet is almost guaranteed to save its owners life someday, which has been a proven otter fact for millions of years.

Once subdued and docile, the human is brought aboard the shuttle and taken to our command ship the Determined Goat 4. Along the way the human is screened for any weapons and anything else that the otter pilots think are fun to play with, and once on the ship, Gobbel's crew does an initial examination of the human. They test to make sure there isn't any brain damage, and then they measure the human's toes and hair length.

The first 3 years Gobbels was on the ship he thought all humans had red hair, but it was just that Derbaron thought it'd be funny to only abduct redheads to mess with the new ott, and everybody but Gobbels thought it was a good joke too.

Anyway, once the toes and hair are measured the serious stuff is out of the way and Gobbels wakes the human up with powerful stimulant drugs he refuses to share with the rest of us. Then the human is fitted with electric diodes so it'll do Gobbels' bidding. Then they make it run on a treadmill and sometimes force it to eat the regenerating banana. The banana incidentally also started as a joke in our early days of genetic engineering. It was modified though. Originally the banana bit the person back, and that's pretty much the whole examination except for the propaganda nature films Gobbels forces the human to watch while under hypnosis.

Having this as my only basis for judging what was to come in this Earth wolf abduction, I was not at ease and seeing as how I was probably in the grasp of sadists, I decided to destroy them with my matter destabilizer. I opened up the survival kit to put it use but discovered that my weapon of defense had been ruined. I wasn't sure when it had been ruined, between the explosion Gomer caused and Gomer's reckless running, but I was sure it was Gomer's fault.

That relieved me of any responsibility, and it wasn't a total loss. All the devices came with a self-destruct, so I could use that to blow up the vehicle, but of course, at that moment I was inside the vehicle and any explosion would also affect me. I thought back on my training and then checked in the OESG.

It was as I thought:

The matter destabilizer included in the indestructible survival kit is to be considered highly sensitive technology, and as such after the first time you use it a timer starts and exactly 13 Earth hours later it will automatically disable itself if the timer is not reset. To reset the timer, drop the matter destabilizer from a height of 8 human feet. If the time does not reset, increase elevation and repeat.

That wasn't what I had thought, but what it told me was something that was nice to know. It would've been nicer to know it sooner as it was completely useless at that point in time, or so I thought until I saw the following:

If you are reading this after having discovered your matter destabilizer disabled, all is not lost. Please read page 1, instruction 3.

With hope of destroying the Earth wolf abductors, I turned to page 1 and read the third instruction:

Read the OESG in its entirety before use of any equipment or you might find yourself reading this after your matter destabilizer has become completely useless.

I looked at Gomer. "Why those dirty... dirty... stotters." I flipped back to the section on the matter destabilizer.

As previously stated, all is not lost. Now you have learned something and next time you're stranded on Earth you will know to reset the timer for your matter destabilizer.

I was getting angry, and got more so as I read on:

Provided you survive your current stranding on Earth.

I scrolled down to where I saw the word 'destruct':

Your matter destabilizer comes equipped with a level 3 self-

destruct mechanism. See 'Destruction Mechanism Levels' for more information.

I flipped forward to the proper section:

Level 1 – Hair remover. Stand back and close your eyes.

Level 2 – Habitat adjuster. The blast will send otter airborne for 15-35ft, depending upon altitude, wind speed, and weight of otter. Stand behind something solid, plug your ears and go into blowfish configuration.

Level 3 – Atlantis killer. Use for small island removal. Be somewhere else underground.

That was as I had thought. The matter destabilizer, being sensitive technology that the humans would find a use for, was fiercely protected and under no conditions would it fall into human hands, and on the off chance it did, the destruction mechanism would see to it that no one in the vicinity lived to tell about it. Of course, that meant that using the destruction mechanism in an enclosed area would not be a good idea. I went back to the section on the matter destabilizer:

The self-destruct on the matter destabilizer will trigger after a certain amount of time. At the time of this writing, proper testing has not been done, so an exact time cannot be stated. At the time of this writing a group of ten matter destabilizers are being tested, and while six have destructed the other four have not. According to the otters working on it, the blast could come anywhere from 33.5235 seconds after the matter destabilizer has disabled itself, to 89 Earth days. Their best guess is somewhere in-between, but they wouldn't make that bet if they could avoid it.

I was indeed in possession of a book written by an otter. "Classic," I told Gomer, "Just classic." When I got back to the ship I would have to remember to find out who it was that thought the matter destabilizer self-disarming function was a funny idea, and then demonstrate how much I disagreed.

Parting

Another idea occurred to me. There was another device in the survival kit: the ultrasound. What the ultrasound does is pick up the faintest of noises and amplify them. Also, it can be set to screen out background noise like annoying human music.

I took out the device and turned it on. It made a beeping sound, which attracted Gomer, so I had to fight him off before I could use it. To do that, I pointed the end with the spring antennae at the two humans. Instantly three patterns of sound appeared on the ultrasound, but I couldn't hear anything. I put on the earphones and picked through the sounds until I had isolated the sound pattern of the music. I muted it and began listening to the conversation.

"I don't know why I bother watching the Twins anymore. Getting as bad as the Vikings."

"C'mon, Frank. Somebody's got to lose."

"Whatever you say, Bill. Pull your hat down, your cheesehead is showing."

There was a pause in the conversation as the fat humans laughed. I didn't understand why but guessed it had something to do with their eating habits as food had been discussed.

"So Frank. What'd you think about old yappy back there?"

I quickly assumed 'yappy' was Gomer.

"Ah, he's got a collar. He'll be home tonight. Dern people should keep their dog on a lease." I took that to mean that Gomer was in good hands, and wouldn't be harmed. I got the impression his human masters were assumed to want him back. This struck me as strange, but then what did I know about humans being the Head of Human Psychology. "You know who I blame? All these morons that grew up on Lassie."

"Yeah."

"Hey Bill, you feel like driving a bit?"

"Sure Frank. Why?"

"Cause," Frank hummed, "I'm thinking, these commies leave their dog run loose, and they expect to just come down and find him at the local animal refuge. What'd you say we bring him downtown to the shelter? Say we found him in their area while we were hitting up Chipotle down there by the place where we were at the other day with the, you know, whatever that thing was with the whatchamacallit on its head."

"Yeah, yeah, the thing on the head there. I remember that,

so all the way down then? Make the jerks go farther?"

"Yeah."

"Sounds good, Frank. Good thinking."

"Thanks, Bill."

I was beginning to like these humans, but then a rather large human transport vehicle passed the vehicle I was in, creating a loud noise that didn't match the sound patterns that I'd muted. so that noise came through the headphones amplified and nearly killed me.

Fortunately, the headphones detached when my head slammed against the wall, so I peacefully woke up some time later. The vehicle cage I was in had stopped moving. I could tell because I was no longer feeling the tremors of its engine. I could say I didn't hear the engine, but at that moment, I couldn't hear anything.

It's almost a chronic condition in my case. Perhaps you're familiar with the fact that explosions are amplified underwater. Well, I am and so were my friends when I was an otterling. We were all fond of swimming in rivers, and at that time firecrackers were legal and many a time I found my ears ringing, but as with otter polo, I usually gave out more than I got.

Getting up off the floor I arranged my survival kit and began to wait. Gomer couldn't see me, but knowing I was there he sniffed around and pawed at the ground. I watched him letting my mind wander.

All things considered, Gomer wasn't such a bad pet. I'd never had one while I was growing up, but my friend Poe had a loop monkey named Monkeyoloto the Drunken Master.

Loop monkeys, or loopeys, are the main pets available on Revir. Older otters think it's healthier for otterlings to watch the loopeys instead of the HoloV, and I'm not sure if that's true, but it does follow my personal guideline in life that anything is better when a computer isn't involved.

HoloV's are a pain to deal with because the computer likes to change the channel every so often, and usually right at the good part. Not a problem with loopeys. You just feed them Iky tree nuts and they spin in circles and sometimes fall out of the tree or whatever they're standing on. My uncle Asimov is a loopey veterinarian, and Poe and I would always bring Monkeyoloto the Drunken Master to him when he fell out of the tree and got hurt. Uncle Asimov would always slap us and offer to buy us a defanged weasel.

Defanged weasels are the second most popular pets on Revir, but whereas the whole family can enjoy a loopey, the weasels are just for otterlings, and the biggest problem with them is that they tend to fight to the death, and so either the weasel or the otterling doesn't last long. Oh, there are cases where a weasel is docile and sociable, which the marketers for the defanged weasels always use for their sale's pitch, but they're the exception, like an otter that the computers like.

And there's no real point in having a nice weasel around anyway. Otters have weasels because they're the perfect size for otterlings to wrestle with, as long as the weasel is defanged. Happens every so often that a fanged weasel gets sold, but so far there haven't been any otterling fatalities because the parent otters tend to play with anything that comes into the house before the otterlings, and so the adult otter finds out quickly if the weasel has fangs.

Weasels are a pain to control too. They're slippery little devils. An entire room has to be set aside to keep the weasel, and it can't have any holes in the walls. Then the otterling, when it wants to play, goes through the wall with a shield barrier calibrated to block the weasel.

Loopeys are much better. All they need is a platform to do circles on and fall off of, and they don't even need a litter box because if you paint something within throwing distance red, the loopey will automatically throw its feces at it. It's otter tradition in most places to paint a red circle on the least favorite neighbor's house the very day a loopey is purchased, and half the time no feces even get thrown.

It's just one of those traditions that's more about just the joy of doing it rather than anything formal. Painting the red circle sends a message to everyone that the otters in this house are the otters you'd most like to have your loopey throw its feces at, and gestures of such beauty are what otter culture is really built on, and oh sure you can say it's not very nice but getting a red circle on your house is just as exciting as putting one on another house. It means that out of all the otter dwellings in the loopey's throwing distance, the loopey owners singled you out as being the worthy one for the red circle.

It's a badge, and with some imagination it can be a badge of honor. It's like winning the lottery in a way that makes you be careful about where you walk and how long you stand still in your backyard because some day you're going to forget and wear a red shirt to work and that loopey is going to nail you ten feet out of the door, and it will take a few years to be able to appreciate the humor in it but everyone else that sees it will laugh right away, and that's the point. There will be more joy in the world, and that's what loopeys do for us otters.

And then there are the beavers. You can't really call them pets but beaver wrestling used to be a tradition. Upon graduation from mandatory schooling, all the otter's relatives would chip in for the shuttle fare to and from Nawiat where the otter could wrestle all the beavers he wanted. Now we can't do that because of the wolves, or at least we otters completely deny any responsibility for any single otter that happens to go Nawiat under his own free will.

It's a good example that there is always a way, and for prime fighting you almost need a beaver, and it's not a simple dynamic to replicate. We still haven't found a good substitute. There are other things to wrestle besides beavers, but none of them work as well. It's a problem of balance.

What is needed is something relatively the same size as an otter, and something that will put up a good fight, but not too good a fight. The goat was thought to be a good substitute, but goats only seem to charge when the otter isn't looking, so that was no good. We tried using young wolves for a while, it was an exchange program with the Pack, but they put up too good a fight. Then we genetically engineered a weasel to make it larger, but that was even worse. Three years ago the Man sent some animals from Earth to try out: bobcat, wolverine, Tasmanian devil, wild boar, komodo dragon and electric eel.

All were failures except for the electric eel, which is now

used to punish the leaders of the upper ranks of disobedient teenage otters.

Our problem is that most of these species don't know the difference between play fighting and killing. All the smaller predatory animals try to get away until they're cornered, and then they do their best to rip apart the otter to get away, and they're mean about it. They fight like females biting and clawing. I remember how Derbaron looked after capturing that wolverine thing. I thought he'd finally crashed a shuttle.

And that's the problem. All these animals don't know how to take a joke. Not that the beavers were any better; in order to get them to fight you had to catch them in their den. What made them great wrestle mates was that they were balanced in fights with otters. They're hard to hurt but slow and they can't do lots of damage right away so it's a safe casual fight.

We otters could fight each other, and we do, but we can do that any time and the experience is still lacking. Fighting a beaver has a different feeling. Fighting an otter you hold back to make sure you don't do too much damage. Beavers you usually don't have to worry because you really want to hurt the dirty dam builder just by pure primal otter instinct.

Watching Gomer I also thought about the beaver suits in development. When they're done otters will take turns wearing the suit and fighting their friends, but about then I lost patience waiting for the door to open, and just after that Gomer, during his sniffing search, found my tail and bit it. I shooed him away and went back to thinking.

I think a pet is what the humans had in mind when they subjugated the Earth wolves. It was much the same as we tried to do with the Pack wolf pup exchange program. Because the wolves were smart we thought we could get the little ones to fight with us nicely, but they ended up being poor losers. No matter what we tried, once the wolf pup got the hang of the fighting, it wouldn't lose.

Gomer had followed me a long distance, he'd disregarded all the sticks and rocks I'd thrown at him, and he'd provided transport. He seemed more than willing to do whatever I wanted to do as long as I fried the brain of a bird or two for him to eat. He was a ready and willing companion. In some way of thinking, I suppose he could be considered dependable, as he never wavered from his unique manner of fumbling everywhere like an intent tube of some chunky yet jello-like substance with fur all over it, with a tongue and nose on one end and a tail on the other, and he reminded me of an otter so deeply in love that he or she couldn't see the evil in his or her mate.

But I couldn't think of Gomer as a pet. He was more of friend, but not an equal friend, more of a clumsy friend I'd hang around with waiting for him to hurt himself in an entertaining fashion. After the doors to the cage opened and the two humans, Frank and Bill, took Gomer out, I felt a twinge of sadness at seeing Gomer the Earth wolf leaving my life. And with that, I descended from the cage and found myself in the middle of a human city.

CITY OTTER

OESG Note on Cities:

The recent outbreak of human cities is possibly evidence of a subconscious human desire to mimic the tree dweeling life of their evolutionary ancestors, like the tailbone but higher up the spine and imaginary inside the head instead of physical.

Chapter 4

Surrounded

The first thing I noticed after walking away from the Earth wolf abduction vehicle was that there were a lot of humans, and I was in danger of being stepped on. On the walkways, there were too many obstacles to navigate through, and in the areas between the walkways, there were humans driving motorized vehicles of various shapes and degrees of noise.

I was out of place, to say the least, not only spatially but also mentally. In essence, I didn't know where I was, but my brain was telling me that wherever I was, was a bad place for me to be. Finding solace in a minor roadway that was about as dirty as my bedroom back in college days, I thought about my predicament.

I was lost without a map. That meant that wherever the Como Zoo was, I didn't know how to get there. That meant that I was lost and needed a map that showed my current position and the position of the Como Zoo. Establishing that need I was still lost without a map.

This frustrated me, so I resorted to instinct and made a conscious decision to completely ignore the problem and distract myself. This wasn't difficult since I was hungry, and I still had my neural destabilizer to play with. Or so I thought.

Knowing I had thought the same thing about the matter destabilizer I decided to make sure my neural destabilizer was still operational. Setting it to stupidity, which would only temporarily disable the higher thought functions of whoever was in the path of the ray, I aimed the device toward the sky and watched the display readings for power usage and output. I clicked off several shots, and then adjusted the beam so it had a wider disbursement, and fired again.

It was about that time I noticed a 'thwock thwock thwock' sound coming from above. I looked up to see I was pointing the neural destabilizer at a human aircraft. I flipped the OESG to the section on human transportation.

COLLATERAL DAMAGE

Ze helicopter crash iz confirmed... and now I vill be observing a moment of silence to honor a fellow pilot.

It's about time he broke something in that city. Send me the video.

Scanning the illustrations I found a match:

Helicopter, Chopper, Copter – an aircraft characterized by a set of rotating propellers mounted on the vehicle providing lift and making flight possible. Used by humans for military actions and surveillance of other humans.

Note - Occasionally involved in the practice of golf.

Knowing that, I looked up and watched the helicopter spiral out of control and proceed to spin in circles in the air. Then it passed out of my view behind one of the large buildings and a short time after I heard the sound of a distant explosion.

Not remembering seeing that under the normal uses for helicopters I reread the OESG. I then began to wonder if my firing the neural destabilizer had anything to do with the explosion and the loud sirens I was suddenly hearing.

For safety's sake, I pointed the neural destabilizer at one of the automobiles on the street and fired. The car quickly swerved into the other lane of traffic and after it passed out of my view I heard a crunching sound and then more horns.

I decided the neural destabilizer worked, and I was the cause of some amount of damage. After chuckling to myself I felt bad about the helicopter. The neural destabilizer was a good joke, but the helicopter was going too far.

Vowing to only use the neural destabilizer on ground-based human vehicles I started squeezing off more shots at the cars in view. I would fire, wait for the telltale sound of a collision for a moment, and if it didn't come I'd fire it again.

Then I heard a beep and looked at the neural destabilizer.

"Power level low. Reduce disbursement."

I reduced the disbursement and using another instinctual otter reaction, started walking down the side walkway away from the damage I'd recently caused. Reaching the other end I spied trees. It seemed the humans, in their crusade to tar over everything natural, had missed a spot. I waited at the side of the walkway for a gap in the passing automobiles.

After about 30 seconds I got frustrated and shot the driver of one automobile with the neural destabilizer. That automobile turned directly into another automobile that wasn't moving and I got to hear that sound of car crashing against car again. This served to considerably slow the flow of automobiles, and I was able to shuffle peacefully to the other side of the road to the treed area.

I thought about sitting on one of the benches placed underneath the trees for just that purpose, but I decided instead to climb one of the trees in order to get a better view. I accomplished this with the same device from my survival kit that I used to attach myself to Gomer: the rope. Of course, the rope alone wasn't much use, I needed something to get the rope attached somewhere up the tree.

I thought about this for a moment, weighing possibilities, but soon all the child humans running around began to annoy me, so I used the first idea that had come to mind. I took one of the garbage bins and pulled it over underneath a tree branch. Then I put rocks underneath it so it was leaning at an angle toward the tree branch. Then I attached the rope to it.

Finally, I sorted through my survival kit looking for the most useless device. I decided on the emergency fire extinguisher since I couldn't imagine I'd ever use one, and I was glad to find it because it was a difficult choice between the other items: my scent detector and PHESA (Personal Handheld Electric Shock Administrator).

I wanted to hang onto the scent detector because I was hungry, and I decided to keep the PHESA because the battery on my neural destabilizer was getting low and a backup weapon is never a bad idea.

So, taking the emergency fire extinguisher, I turned on its self-destruct mechanism and placed it underneath the garbage receptacle. I was hoping the explosion, which was only a level 1.7439, would be sufficient to send the garbage receptacle over the tree branch. The rope attached to the receptacle was then supposed to follow it over the tree branch and I left a lot of slack on the rope so I wasn't worried about the receptacle flying too far and overshooting the mark.

The fire extinguisher exploded nicely, sending a heavy spray of concentrated white form over some of the children playing nearby, and the garbage receptacle went into the air. I'm sure you don't expect everything to have worked out correctly, and yes, unfortunately, I had badly aimed the receptacle and instead of flying over the tree branch, it crashed into it and ricocheted off toward the roadway where it landed on the men assembled to see to the car that I had helped crash.

The people looked surprised at first with the loud noise, the shower of garbage over the area, the white children running around screaming and then the garbage receptacle falling gracefully from the sky and embedding itself in the roof of one of the automobiles, but amazingly after a few minutes of trying to explain the freak occurrence the humans went back to what they were doing, except for the suddenly white child humans who were taken away by their mothers.

The good part of all this was that the branch had cracked in half and now provided an easy means of climbing up into the tree. I did so and began to take in the scene.

What I said before about it being strange that everyone went back to what they were doing was true. It was strange, and the longer I sat in the tree watching the humans the stranger things became.

First of all, I couldn't imagine where all these people were going. They were all moving, and moving very quickly, so I assumed they were on their way to someplace important to do something important, but I had no idea what it was. Some were in cars, some were walking, and others were tempting death by riding on some two-wheeled contraptions that required the driver to pedal.

Everyone was busy. I was getting depressed watching all the commotion. It was bringing back nightmares I was plagued with as a child, which were brought on by my father's stories of his escapades on the beaver planet. According to him, which is by no means to be considered true, the beavers were the same way, always running or swimming around chewing on trees and maneuvering them into place.

That was all beavers did according to my father, and every time I accidentally destroyed some of his property I remembered those stories, and then I ceased feeling bad.

There was no amount of property I could destroy that would make up for the trauma he'd caused me with his tales, and the underlying idea they contained; that stories about beavers could teach an otterling something, a theory disproved easily by advanced otter reasoning.

Truly, a terrible thing to do to an otterling, and I would just like to give a shout out here to my otts in Otters Traumatized by PBS, or Parent Beaver Stories. Thank you all, you've always been otters that would let me whine for hours about my life without making fun of me, even though I've always made fun of all of you, basically constantly all this time, and occasionally I've used overheard information to do what some would describe as blackmail, and seriously otts, I don't understand any of you at all.

You, my friends, are all like another species to me, and that's fine, but if you ask me you should all be committed, and I just wanted to let you know that because I've said it before and a few otters out there who know who they are don't seem to take me seriously, and I'm tired of it to tell the truth.

So in keeping with the Treaty of Class Action I'm letting all you OTPBSers out there know that you should all start watching your backs, and by certifying my intent here in published writing I can now go about my plans with Full Mischief Capacity and here's a hint; yodeling loopeys throwing blocks of ice at goats painted the blackest hue of a place far underground without electricity.

Beware and prepare.

Apprenticeship

Not far from the tree I was sitting in I noticed a strangely painted human acting out some hideous dance. He was black and white, and seemed to be trapped inside of a force field of some sort, but his manner of addressing the problem made me think he enjoyed it. I quickly looked up human behavior patterns in the OESG and found a match for the odd human:

Mime - a lunatic human who is capable of causing great harm by functioning as a symbol of racial divide or good versus evil, leading the weak of mind to question their morals and thus cause friction within society. Disable if possible.

I sighted him with my neural destabilizer and popped him with a nice prolonged dose. He immediately fell upon his face and some of the remaining child humans began throwing rocks at him. I laughed for a moment, but my heart wasn't in it. I had too many worries in my mind and I was still hungry.

Then I noticed another circle of humans, gathered around a man that repeatedly threw strange objects into the air and caught them. I checked the OESG.

Juggler – entertainers suspected of doubling as secret agents for subversive groups. Avoid.

I sniffed a laugh at the OESG entry and then shot the juggler with the neural destabilizer. Six pieces of fruit flew through the air and into splatting situations with the onlookers. Laughing again, I felt a grumbling in my stomach. I was very hungry, and the time had come to do something about it.

I prepared to get down from my perch when I spied another odd human. Against my better judgment, I checked the OESG.

Bum, homeless person, hobo, vagrant – a group of well-organized crime lords responsible for the majority of creative commerce on Earth.

Note - the only group of humans besides politicians having mastered a means of living without working.

Foolishly believing the OESG I thought I'd found the map I needed. I descended from the tree to investigate the matter. My hopes were high, but assuming that a human who had managed to outsmart all the other humans was a dangerous animal, I kept my distance. Also, an unpleasant smell increased in unpleasantness the closer I got to the bum.

I sat there studying the creature, and occasionally zapping a human child that got too near with my PHESA. I looked at the bum intensely, seeking to find the quality that made him superior to the other humans, and possibly to discover some way to safely make contact with the smelly man.

The bum was dirtier than the average human but less so than Gomer. He wore a drab green overcoat, had lots of facial hair that covered the majority of his face and wore an odd pair of goggles, or half a pair since the lens from the right side was missing. His formal attire and bodily decorations had obviously taken a large amount of work. I found it all very curious. In front of him was a cloth container with pieces of metal inside it. I looked at the OESG for more insight:

Coins – stored by humans in their pockets for the purpose of adding texture to the outline of their clothing.

My suspicions grew as I read the next entry:

These pocket liners are in high demand depending upon the area of Earth. Many humans are willing to exchange these metal pieces for food, clothing, or other pieces of metal.

The reason my suspicions were raised was because the entry seemed much too factual to be true and by factual I mean sounding like the truth. It goes back to Otter Psychology, and I'm not versed in that so I can't explain it, but I would guess that it's about being interesting. Factual information is not interesting, and when presented with uninteresting factual information an otter is almost duty bound to alter it and make it interesting.

If the information in the OESG portrayed the true purpose of the coins, I was certain any otter, and especially an otter that wrote for a living would've taken the opportunity to misinform the reader. It would've simply been far too good to pass up, and an editor going through the book would undoubtedly fire an otter for including something that factual and boring, unless of course, it wasn't true. That's the other side of the coin, as it were.

Factual information is fine and good, as long as it isn't true, and this trend of problems with communication in otter society can be best shown by considering the computers. At the age of six, every otter goes through a test to see if they have the personality required for computer work. It's a fairly simple process. The young otter goes up to a computer and requests some information that is common knowledge. At that point, the computer, analyzing the words used and the pitch of the otter's voice, will either give the correct information or a load of complete weasel fur. Then the otter will be told to ask for the information a second time.

That was when my test ended, as is the case with most otters. At that point, I slammed my fist on the computer screen and the failure siren went off. Actually, I don't know what happens if the information is requested a second time. I've never met anyone that wasn't either accepted on the first attempt or tried to smash the computer, and Otter Psychology states that otters are stable in their extremism, and whatever that means we've been using it as an excuse for all kinds of things for a long time now, and most otters find it to be good wisdom and not because we know what it means but just because it's practical, as in, it works as an excuse.

As I sat watching, a passing human dropped some coins into the bag in front of the bum with the other coins. I felt this was an important event, but couldn't figure out why. The entire time the bum hadn't moved, in fact, he hadn't moved since I started watching him. He just sat there gazing absently toward an older human woman that was throwing crumbs of food at some dirty looking gray birds. I couldn't figure out how he'd managed to get the passing human to give up the coins.

And then it hit me. I could shoot the dirty birds with my neural destabilizer. I took it out and began firing. At first, it had no effect, but then the birds all at once took to the air and several crashed into trees.

As I sat giggling I felt another rumble in my stomach, and then the solution to the matter hit me, and it had nothing to do with the dirty birds; it had everything to do with the dirty bum.

Becoming Human

The beaver suit project wasn't started with the intention of substituting a disguised otter for a beaver for the purpose of entertainment fighting. At the project's beginning there was a full-scale war going on, or what passed for one, and so there was no shortage of fighting partners.

The problem the beaver suits were meant to solve was espionage. There were a lot of otters trained in espionage and stationed on the beaver world, but the majority of them were captured after their first day of duty because all the espionage training couldn't hinder the normal otter instinct to rush and fight the first beaver it saw, or in the case of the spy otters, to shout insults at them from the top of a hill or wherever else the otter was supposed to be hiding.

Needless to say, that gave away the spy's position and shortly after the beavers would arrest the otter, and a new spy would be needed, but the beaver suit was supposed to solve all that. You see, spying is too concealed and boring for an otter to get interested in. We otters can't stand being detached from what's going on, and with spying all you do is watch what happens, and even worse all there was to see was a bunch of beavers kissing trees.

But what we can stand, and are willing to put up with, is being quiet long enough to pull off a joke, and walking into a beaver camp dressed as a beaver and getting back out without incident is a pretty good joke. With beaver suits our espionage endeavors would've had a lot more success, but unfortunately, and when dealing with otters there is a lot of 'unfortunately', the Pack stepped in and halted the war before the suits could be perfected but the important thing here is the principle of sneaking around looking like a beaver, and that after shooting the dirty birds I was very hungry.

The realization came from somewhere I suppose, but I didn't catch where, but I suddenly realized that with a little extending of the fur around my mouth, some stretching of my body and some clothes like those of the bum, I could make a human suit. And even better it was a human bum suit, which would obligate the other humans to pander to my desires.

It was more or less amazingly brilliant, and I started right away finding the clothing I would need. It didn't take long to find a store that carried the proper coat. I decided against any of the approaches mentioned in the OESG and simply stuffed the coat into my survival kit.

Then I obtained some of the large pants I'd seen some of the younger humans wearing. I didn't bother with shoes since the large pants tended to cover the feet.

As walked out of the clothing store behind a female human with two children, an alarm sounded. As I continued down the walkway, I glanced back to see the woman being hassled by an employee from the clothing store. I stopped and continued to watch as her children were searched and she was subjected to verbal abuse.

There was a lot of verbal abuse going on when an automobile with flashing lights arrived. I noticed the other cars on the roadway pulled aside for the flashy car and out of it stepped a man in uniform, and he seemed to take charge of the situation.

I could see clearly what was going on. Someone had called the human version of the rats, which was the slang term my father and his peers used during the time of the otter police force, which was intensely unpopular during its short existence.

The rats were a provision in the treaty the Pack made us sign with the beavers. The Pack seemed to think that our lack of a public security force was a bad thing, and every so often they make us do something idiotic to make us less destructive and one time they made us create the rats, but the experiment only lasted for five years. Once the wolves stopped paying attention we secretly gave up on the idea, which is standard procedure when dealing with Pack orders.

We've never really felt the need for a public security force. Otter society has always revolved around responsibility and independence, so we barely support people telling us what rules are, and there's no way we're going to like anyone that makes us follow the law.

And it's so unnecessary. Take crime for instance. If one otter assaults another otter, the simplest way to resolve the situation is for the attacked otter to gather all his family, friends, and coworkers and go beat the snot out of the attacking otter. Naturally the attacking otter will then rally his own friends, family, and coworkers for defense.

Anytime you get that many male otters together at least half of them are going to be married or still under the control of their mothers, and the females, or ottays, will assume the males, or ottyos, are expecting them to cook for the entire group of otters and the females will take exception to that and thoroughly scold their mates and sons, and then those otters will be forced to withdraw from the big fight. About that time too the word goes around the female circles about the males that are fighting, and any females that knows the fighting males will start to scold them, and finding work for them to do around the house instead, and then after about a week the males will decide that things were better before they started fighting, or less total work, and then they'll make peace.

And every so often the male otters remember what'll happen if they cause trouble and so they won't take the risk without proper provocation and in general revenge is proper; defense against revenge is not. That means that the initial attacking otter will find himself without friends when the attacked otter's family, friends, and coworkers come to knock the beaver out of him.

That's basically how peace has always been kept between otters. Besides, we males are usually too busy to bother holding a grudge, and when we're frustrated there's always a game of otter polo not too far out of the way and in the end no otter likes to see rules followed, including the rats, who spent most of their time eating donuts and drinking coffee.

As I was walking away from a potential problem, namely the human rat, I glanced in the windows of the other stores. Looking into the window of a store called Zannini's Magic and Jokes I became interested.

I waited outside the door for someone to enter the store so I could follow. No one was going in or coming out, and I was getting impatient, so I used my neural destabilizer on the clerk. After the man collapsed on the floor I went inside and made an acquisition.

What I acquired were two items that would complete my human suit: a large hat, and a pair of glasses that came equipped not only with a fake nose, but also a fake mustache. Its brims were exquisitely black and large, and the nose was a soft flesh-toned peach. I was so excited I began to assemble my disguise right then, although I kept myself cloaked.

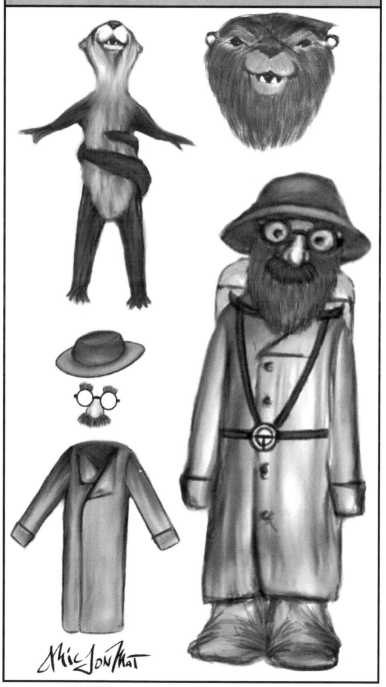

First, I experimented pulling air into the tendons of my legs and arms so that the jacket would fit. Then I made the fur around my mouth grow to a length proportional to that of the bum I'd seen. Those were the easy parts.

I found that the glasses with nose and mustache were not suited to my head shape, so I had to change my facial curves, making the ears lower and on level with the eyes. That took a long time to get right. I also decided to make the rest of the hair on my head grow longer to cover my ears, and turn my fur to change its color so I only looked scruffy around the eyes instead of my normal beautiful full furred look, a necessary ugliness. And then I had it. I was immaculately disguised as a vagrant, and quite pleased with myself. Then my pants fell down. Using another rope from the survival kit I managed to get them to stay up, and with my leg wear properly supported I was ready to go out into the world and eat.

Sustenance

Hoping to pass as a human I wandered out of the store, turned off my cloaking device, and began a search for someplace to eat. In my haste and hunger, it was some time before I realized that I was now walking among the hairless monkeys as one of them, albeit a hairy one.

This was important to realize because I was no longer hidden from view, and as such would be responsible for my actions. I realized this as I was pulling the neural destabilizer out of my pocket to cause another automobile crash so I could easily cross the road. Realizing it wouldn't be a good idea, I left the neural destabilizer where it was and waited with the humans at the roadway intersection.

It was there I noticed that the intersection was equipped with some form of traffic control system that used warning lights. When a red light was shown, automobiles stopped their forward movement and waited for a green light before proceeding. A yellow light came on as well, but I couldn't figure out what it was for because different humans reacted differently to it.

Naturally I felt an urge to go against the grain of the traffic, to keep going when the light was red. I don't know where this urge came from, but it came immediately when I realized the light's purpose.

Walking across the street I forgot about the lights and concentrated on my hunger. I debated asking one of the humans where food, namely fish, could be acquired, but the humans around me seemed to be wary. They looked at me strangely or better said they didn't look. They kept their distance, as if there was something wrong with me.

I attributed this to the general distrust of authority that must exist in the human world. Personally I hoped it didn't exist, because if it didn't then I couldn't imagine there being any hope for the humans, and that's good for us otters, but unfortunately distrust of authorities did seem present and I assumed that because I was dressed as a bum, a marked upper authority figure of human society, the normal working class humans were simply wary of my presence.

I wondered if they were in fear of me for a good reason or just out of superstition. Possibly there was some hidden talent or power the bums held that brought about this fear, and if there was I wanted to know what it was so I could have some fun with it.

I told myself I could think about it later; after I'd eaten. So I took out my scent detector and set it for fish. The fish compass began going wild and then pointed at a building with two large yellow arches in its name. It was called McDonald's. I couldn't imagine there was fish there because I couldn't smell fish and I have a good nose, but I went to check it out.

Nearing the building I kept my senses tuned for what was going on. I didn't want to attract attention to myself now that I was uncloaked, and I had no real expectation of how I would handle the procedure for food requisition. In need of advice, I checked the OESG:

Food service locations, restaurants, diners – places where food can be obtained.

Finding no advice I put the OESG away and took a step toward the building. I would have to make it up as I went.

Initially, before anything happened, I panicked. The door to the building wouldn't budge. Worrying that a computer was controlling the door I took out my PHESA to destroy it, but then I remembered the humans had nice computers. Then I noticed a handle on the door and pulled. The door came open. I put my PHESA away.

Inside looked clean, or looked like it was trying to look clean. The tile floors were cold as I shuffled across them with my pants. Around the walls were advertisements for strange artificial looking products. They were mostly shaped like squished orbs, but nearly all of them had a rotten green leafy substance stuck between two brown indistinguishable substances. I saw nothing that looked remotely like a fish.

Troubling me greatly was what I took to be a real person dressed remotely like the mime character from the park. It had a painted face and bright ridiculous clothing. But watching it for a moment I realized it was just a statue.

Looking in the OESG I found this entry:

Clown – a mythical monster often used by humans to scare their children into unconsciousness.

Worried I continued shuffling away from the clown, looking for something that looked like a fish. A young female human behind a metal counter was watching me. When she noticed that I noticed that she was watching me she didn't behave in the usual manner for a peeping tom. She spoke up.

She asked, "Can I help you, Sir?"

I recognized the word 'sir' as a formal term for someone of rank. I was obviously receiving special treatment because of my bum status. "Fish please," I said happily.

She frowned at me. "Could you speak up, Sir?"

"Um…I'd like some fish," I articulated as best I could.

"Fish?" She repeated. "A fish fillet?"

"Sure," I answered, not really sure what she'd asked. I could barely hear her from where I was next to the wall.

"Excuse me, Sir?"

"Why? What'd you do?"

"Could you come here, Sir?"

"Sure." I walked over to the counter and waited for her to speak.

"Would you like a fish fillet value meal or just the sandwich?"

I sighed trying to look like I was weighing intelligently the options. "What's a sandwich?"

Her mouth opened and stayed open. "Um… a sandwich." She gestured with her hands. "It's fish inside of bread."

"Oh, that'd be fine," I said nodding. "As long as it's fish."

"Okay," she smiled. She began punching numbers on a computer and then looked up at me. "Would you like anything to drink with that?"

I thought that was a silly question. All fish come with water inside of them unless they're overly cooked. "No, I'll just eat the fish."

While she worked with the computer I began to wonder if the fish I was being given was going to be fresh or if it'd be cooked. There's a big difference between cooked and uncooked fish. Most otters prefer the latter kind, but we try to respect those that would rather have their fish cooked, but that's just currently and in the past it was a capital offense to cook fish. I myself don't mind cooked fish, but if given the choice I'd rather have it raw. I was about to ask the female human if the fish would be cooked when she spoke again.

"That'll be 3.32, please."

I looked at her and said, "Okay. Great."

She smiled as if I'd made a joke. "That'll be 3.32, please."

"3.32 what?"

She laughed as if I'd made another joke. "Dollars," she said slowly.

I nodded as if I now understood. "What are dollars?"

"Money."

"Oh."

She quit smiling. "Um." She began looking around for something. "Um…do you have 3 dollars and 32 cents?"

I thought about it and replied, "Not that I'm aware of."

She looked down at her computer and shook her head. "I need 3.32 to sell you a fish sandwich, Sir."

"Oh. Where can I-," and then it hit me; the coins the other humans gave the bum I saw in the park were money. Money was required to buy food. I began to understand the system, even though it didn't make sense.

Apparently the humans would give money to bums in order for them to buy food, but the restaurants would not give away the food without the money. As I thought about it I realized that it made sense. By forcing the bum's to obtain money or coins, the humans were, in fact, forcing them to do their work, which if nothing else would keep them in training. Money was actually a primitive system for making sure the upper class of society did its job.

It was very different from the system we otters use. We use other ways to know if our rulers are doing their jobs, which are to keep us supplied with everything we want, or at least the potential to work to get everything we want. So when one of us notices a potential amusement, service, or product is not available, then that otter calls for a revolution.

When I say services, I'm talking about luxuries. Our basic needs are free, like food for example. Fish are free to whoever can catch them. That's why all our spaceships and buildings come equipped with a hatchery and pool so that during lunch breaks otters can go and catch their fish. That's a basic need, and it's free.

All the extra fun stuff we have to do for ourselves, and for most of those activities, we use slapping, which works very well. The basic principle is that the otter working to provide a service for other otters charges a slapping admission. For instance, a trip to the beaver planet used to cost 18 slaps a day for the trip's duration and in practice that meant that whenever the otters transporting the passengers felt like having some fun the passengers let them hit them because they were providing the service of transport from one location to another.

That is how all purchases are made. It was reasoned at one point that the best way to place value on a product or service is by how much pain an otter is willing to put up with to get that product or service. That way everything has a price and that way no otter ever has more wealth than the next because we all have roughly same tolerance for pain.

The human system, while less interesting, was no less

complicated, and I had much to learn of the ways of humans.

"I'll go get some money," I instructed the female human. "Just keep the fish alive until I get back."

With that, I left the building in search of money.

Commerce

I began to realize that the special power of the bums, however they managed to get the other humans to give them money, was a power I did not possess. It was fairly simple, and I used the otter logic of starting at the end to figure it out.

I wanted to eat, to get the fish from the clown restaurant. That was the end result I was looking for. To get to that end result I needed money. To get the money I needed to get people to give it to me. To get people to give it to me I needed to know how to get people to give it to me.

To find out how to get people to give me money, the logical place to start was with the bum from the park. So I went back to the park.

As I once again came across the treed area, I was in a good mood. I felt as if I was playing one of the games from my childhood, like 'steal the fish from the otter with the otter polo mallet' or 'how high can the box containing an unknown object be dropped without breaking the unknown object inside'. These were fond memories, and they were so powerful that I managed to ignore my hunger.

Sitting down next to the motionless bum I fully expected some sort of greeting as I had the appearance of one of his kind. I wondered if he might try to expose me as an impostor, so I kept my hand on my cloaking device.

Suddenly, the bum moved. Suddenly, the bum spoke, "Hey, buddy!"

"Yes?"

"Go work somewhere else. This is my spot."

"Oh," I said apologetically. There was obviously a complex system of territories associated with working as a bum. It made so much sense I should've thought of it before. There's no need for two presidents of one country after all.

Apologizing again I went to the other end of the park and

sat down next to the walkway. I placed my survival kit in front of me, making sure to keep everything inside hidden, and then awaited the money.

After about a half Earth hour, no money had come, and I was confused. I was obviously lacking the talent for getting the contributions. Sitting there wasn't doing me any good, and every minute I became more and more conscious of how hungry I was.

I walked back to the bum to see what I could learn from the man.

"Hello," I said.

"What?" He grumbled.

"I'm having a problem."

"What's that?"

"I'm not getting any money."

The bum laughed. "It takes patience."

That posed a problem. "I don't have any patience."

He laughed again. "Then do something."

"I was doing something," I replied. "I was sitting over there."

"Try doing something else."

"Like what?"

"Do you play any music?"

"No, computers don't like me."

"What? Whatever, how about singing? Can you sing?"

"Sing? I don't…oh…singing. I see. I can do that."

I felt I had found a piece to the puzzle. It's been known for centuries that music affects the moods of all living creatures, and although unknown to otter science it was indeed possible that by playing music I could move several humans to give money donations.

I assumed playing music was the novice bum technique for obtaining the coins, and through years of observing the dynamics at work, a veteran bum progressed to the master level and had no more need of devices to get money, achieving it instead by pure force of will.

I thanked the bum and walked over toward my spot in the park. Getting back to my spot I noticed a pair of humans, male and female, sitting not far away. They were lying on the grass underneath a tree and were engaged in some cooperative activity that required touching their mouths together. I wondered if I was witnessing some type of human behavior that I was better off not seeing.

Ignoring them I proceeded to produce the greatest music as yet discovered in the universe. The search was a long one, and the one-year course of music history that I took in college was only a survey. That means I can't give specifics, but most specifics are lies anyway.

Otters like music, but we're not that accomplished at it. We play a lot of instruments, but we usually just make noise or end up breaking them. In the early days, we relied on weather formations and waves for our music. Those were just recordings and our played music and singing comes from other worlds, particularly the wolves and dolphins. They're pretty musical, and we're pretty torn between which we prefer.

See, we're part land and part water dwellers, whereas the wolves are on land and the dolphins are in the water. That means that we can appreciate both the styles or more accurately, we can't decide between the two and the popularity of each tends to shift up and down with each generation. It's a well-documented occurrence. If the parents listen to dolphins, the kids will like wolves, and so on. It's a generation thing, and it keeps the music world healthy.

Of course, when we returned to Earth we began finding new music. Taking samples from the animals we found on Earth, the wolves and dolphins both tinkered with the sounds and produced a whole variety of new music and after a long debate and some riots, we otters have finally decided upon a form of music as our national favorite. Likely it'll only last a generation, mine specifically, but that's what I had to work with as I sat down to make music to convince humans to give me money.

And so I started my favorite song.

"Arf Arf Arf Arf Arf Arf Arf."

Otter Music

OESG Note on Music: Previously believed to be one of the many symptoms of GHM (General Human Madness), today human music is understood as an accepted social mechanism for repelling unwanted company, meaning humans who prefer another kind of music.

As you may have guessed, the style of music we otters decided on is a slight alteration of the singing of seals. I continued singing for about five minutes without effect. This worried me a little. The passing humans had stopped passing. They were now giving me a wide berth in their travels. There were a few staring at me, but no one was giving money.

Deciding that the music just needed some time to sink in I started singing again. This time, I was louder and after only ten seconds I got the reaction I was looking for.

The male of the male/female couple underneath the tree shouted, "Hey! If I give ya five bucks will you shut up?"

"What's a buck?"

Truth

Things proceeded well after the male of the male/female couple explained to me that a buck was another word for a dollar and that not all the human money was in coin form. Although he didn't like my singing, the man was very helpful. He explained to me that the food at McDonald's was crap and if I wanted fish I should go to a market a short distance away.

I took his advice gratefully since the clown from McDonald's scared me. Making the trip to the market I was happy again knowing that soon I would be eating. At the market, I chose a fish and gave the man my paper currency, and then I returned to the park proudly carrying my catch.

It was strange simply giving money for the fish. On one hand it was easier, but on the other it was more complicated and on another hand there was something lacking from the experience. That's three hands, which isn't right, which is a good sign there was something else wrong with the fish.

In any case, simply giving the money was an easy act, but getting the money had been more complicated. All told it took almost an Earth hour with all the confusion involved, and in the same amount of time I could've caught and eaten 8 fish, provided there was a properly stocked pool. Also, self-caught fish always taste better.

But I was hungry, and as I sat down on a chair in the park, I didn't care. I ate the fish messily and threw what was left in one of the garbage receptacles. Peacefully fattened and calmed, as we otters say, I sat back on the bench and relaxed. Some child humans were coming towards me and I thought about using the PHESA, but I let out a large burp and that was enough to scare them away.

The sun was shining, and I was beginning to enjoy being a human. It was peaceful, and yet in the back of my mind I knew I'd had to do an unreasonable amount of work in order to achieve that peace, but I was fattened and calmed enough that the thoughts in the back of my mind were very quiet.

Near me on the bench, I noticed some reading material. I thought it'd be a nice break reading something besides the OESG. I picked it up and looked at the first page:

The Biggest Hoax of all Time: The Moon Landings.

I read through the article that put forth an argument that the government of the United States of America had faked moon landings since 1969. Apparently the article's author was sure it was all an elaborate joke played by the Americans to upset some other group of humans named the Russians. It made me laugh because 'america' is Burble for 'slobbering donkey', but otherwise, I didn't see what the big deal was. Going to the moon is about as appealing as getting a beaver tail to the head.

There's nothing on it. It's just a cratered expanse of white powdery rock. There isn't even any air, and there certainly isn't any fun going on there. Revir has two moons, both roughly like Earth's moon, and no otter has ever set foot on either one.

As for any humans landing on Earth's moon, we otters don't know because most of our records for that time were lost, and of course it's completely possible the Otternot crew of the Determined Goat 3 didn't even bother recording something as tedious as a primitive human space program devoting tons of time and energy into something as pointless as leaving a blue paradise planet to hang out on a barren lifeless moon.

The loss of records was the human's fault of course. It was about that time that the abductions were getting weird. All of them seemed to be male humans with lots of hair and carrying odd substances in their possession. These odd substances were roughly similar to the Iky tree nuts that the loopeys liked.

Bench News

No otter has visited either of Revir's two
moons in recorded history, mainly because
they lack water and life and therefore fish.

Just like loopeys, the humans were on drugs and unfortunately, the otters abducting these humans began testing the drugs to discover the effects of the substances. The tests were done by whichever otter happened to confiscate the drugs from the human, and the otter tested them either on her or himself.

Therefore, at the time of the moon landings, most of the Otternots orbiting Earth were out of their minds, and all the information recorded by them has been sealed for at least 200 hundred years, at which time the present government will probably be overthrown and so the otters in charge won't have to worry about looking bad for all the useless information that was gathered.

It's Ed's favorite pastime to try to crack the passwords on those files. He's opened up a few, and those that he's let me read have all pretty much been the same. Those otters were seeing space fish everywhere and spent their time on the drugs chasing the imaginary prey, and then abducting more long-haired humans when the drugs wore off.

I threw the paper into the garbage receptacle because that was where it seemed to fit. Sitting back to relax again I felt as if something was missing. I was dressed as a human, sitting on a park bench, properly fed, and at ease with my inner self. And yet something was missing.

Perhaps it was companionship that I lacked. The day had been a new experience, and I wanted to share those experiences with another otter, to make him or her jealous or to pretend all the pain hadn't bothered me, or at least not made me cry like an otterling. That was probably what I needed, I guessed, another otter to brag about my adventures at until I had digested the fish at which time the other otter would have had enough of listening to me and would be ready to fight.

Perhaps it wasn't company, but a simple distraction that I required. For some reason, the park had quieted down. It looked as if evening was approaching, and most of the child humans had been forcefully removed from the area by their parents. I was starting to enjoy having the child humans around. Sometimes, between running around and screaming, they would trip over things and fall down.

Perhaps it was some visual stimuli that I lacked. At that point in time, I didn't feel like talking, and I didn't feel like fighting. What I wanted was to hear and watch others doing those things. Looking around for some example of this, I noticed a store named, "Guy's Electronics." Through the store's window, I could see a strange box with a picture on it. The picture flashed and changed to another picture.

I stood up from the bench and walked toward the store, where everything went very, very wrong.

Chapter 5

Pure Art

The secrets kept from the Pack and the other intelligent life forms are kept for a very good reason. For the otter rulers to remain in power they have to make sure that the luxuries we have come to rely upon remain available, and many of those luxuries are produced on Earth.

The beautiful music of the seals is only one of the many forms of entertainment that come from Earth, and it isn't even the most popular. Also not the most popular are documentaries that try to explain various human activities like golf. Those are geared towards the highbrow viewers and specially made to be informative and boring so normal otters don't take interest and the field of study can remain elitist.

Other popular but not the most popular exports are the documentaries on the Otternot activities on Earth. In a sense, the heads of many departments on the ships are celebrities back on Revir. I'm not because Human Psychology is dull as mud. Loki from Natural Phenomenon Propagation is probably the hottest at the moment, even though he received a reprimand for taking the Mt. St. Helens too far and blowing it up instead of just making it grow really big.

Following Loki would be Nester from Mythological Creature Propagation, who never ceases to bring back video footage of humans looking really confused when he buzzes their cars with a shuttle or makes a hologram monster jump out at them from behind a tree. Nero from Bird Behavior Altering and Pastor from Disease Manipulation round out the top four, but Pastor is rapidly declining in the public view. He's still riding on a few of his early projects, the ones from the early 70s when he taped his lab assistants using the drugs confiscated from long-haired human, which are technically billed as theater and not reality programming, but those are the heavyweights in the entertainment industry and their exploits are common dinner table talk back on Revir.

And then there are the classic videos, like the one of the snow falling on the dinosaurs, Atlantis blowing up, the black hole crashing into Siberia, the storm that blew the Spanish Armada off course, the otter shuttle accidentally crashing into that Hindenburg blimp thing, the plagues we punished the Egyptians with after they made a bunch of animal gods without making one of the first ten we happened to look at an otter, and the otter shuttle accidentally smashing the nose off that sphinx thing.

Those are just some of the classics, and nearly every otter has them memorized. Most of the stuff we do today doesn't get that kind of attention, but some of the other department heads have achieved a cult following even though their work is pretty boring. Take my archival Mikey Fish, the head of Human Sociology. He makes a show every month to jabber on about some new beaver theory he has about the humans, and loyal groups back on Revir watch it if the HoloV computers will let them.

There's also Poseidon from Weather System Supervision, and I enjoy his hurricane documentaries but whenever I see one of his tornado documentaries it's obvious to me he doesn't really know what he's doing when it comes to the weather.

I don't mean to picky, but his tornadoes rarely touch a human town and never one of the interesting cities, and that is the main criticism of Poseidon back on Revir, so I'm not saying anything new here, I'm just quoting the critics.

But all those exports are secondary to the unchallenged master of otter entertainment, that dirty pilot Derbaron. He is beyond a doubt the otter with his hand on the pulse of what works in entertainment. Because he's the head of the shuttle pilots, he has an advantage over the rest of us. While we work to create and alter and bring about interesting things on Earth, Derbaron just has to sit back and make sure his pilots have their cameras on. Almost magically some humans somewhere are doing something otters consider hilarious, such as crashing their automobiles or crashing their trains or crashing their airplanes or running from burning buildings or getting struck in the head or groin with some flying object.

Derbaron always seems to catch these special moments, probably because the other department heads have to rely on the pilots for their footage so he gets first pick of everything coming off the Earth, and any accidents or disasters caught on tape goes into his personal file and gets sent back to Revir.

Those are the shows the otter rulers have to keep arriving if they want to stay in power. We on the ship know this, and that's really why we bother recording footage. If we become popular back home there's no way we can get fired, but what I was seeing through the window of the electronics store was something different. What I was watching had the potential to revolutionize otter entertainment.

I've seen all of Derbaron's stuff and none of it came close to the three humans I was watching. I immediately recognized their genius as they acted out complicated action sequences with impeccable finesse and spiritually harmonious timing. I sat engrossed by their motions, the words spoken and the fanatical realism in their facial expressions.

As such use of props! The three savants used hammers, mallets, screwdrivers, wrenches, fists, fire hoses, red hot metal, guns, swords and cannons as if the objects were true extensions of their bodies.

Somehow on the crummy little planet Earth, I had discovered a priceless jewel. During the few seconds I was not laughing uncontrollably I was crying from the pain in my stomach. It was beauty beyond measure, a godlike creative act captured in perfect clarity. Then, abruptly, it stopped.

I was using my ultrasound to listen from my side of the glass, and when the great display ended I heard a man say, "The Three Stooges will be right back! Don't touch that dial!"

Disturbance

But the great disciplining Moe, the misunderstood Larry, and the corruptly, beautifully, idiotic Curly, did not come right back. Instead, some perverted form of advertising for some product called 'Viagra' was interrupting the Three Stooges. Not only was this advertisement a completely unwelcome interruption but it was also misleading.

TV DISCOVERY

OESG Note on TV:

Humans employ the television to broadcast a wide range of mostly harmless information for the purpose of automating as much of the childrearing process as possible. Effectiveness is increased when paired with video games.

It started with an automobile traveling fast, and I assumed I was in store for some more hilarious antics of the great stooges, but then some gray-haired old human male appeared speaking about whatever the Viagra thing was and telling me I should consult my doctor and see if Viagra was right for me.

As I was staring blankly ahead, wondering what the beaver Viagra was, another advertisement came on the screen that was as confusing and no less frustrating. It had something to do with a product called Rogaine and again when I reached the end of the advertisement, I had no idea what Rogaine was.

I was becoming annoyed. I looked around for some form of authority to report the store's owner to, but then it occurred to me that advertising might work differently among the humans.

We otters banned all advertising after the Wars of Malice because that was another way some otters found to annoy otter society in general. After most all the computers were smashed the first law that was made was the banning of all interruptions in entertainment. We did away with the silly pauses and timeouts that players in otter polo games used to take advantage of to rest and recuperate, we outlawed the use of logos on products and beat up all the graduates from marketing schools.

Ever since entertainment has been a lot more peaceful and a lot more interesting. The constraints on the advertisers force them to squeeze messages into clips that can be presented quickly and then run away with as the otters who saw the advertisement tend to chase down advertisers and hurt them.

Basically, advertisers are forced to illegally advertise. The preferred method of doing this is at otter polo games and by paying the wolves or dolphins to encode subliminal messages into their music. At the otter polo matches, it's fairly common for an otter with a hologram projector to stand up and broadcast an advertisement for a few seconds. It's so common that the fans at the games spend half the time watching their neighbors for signs of advertising. Then the advertising otter either runs and gets away or gets caught and thrown into the otter polo match where the players take a pause from the hallowed sporting event to administer a beating.

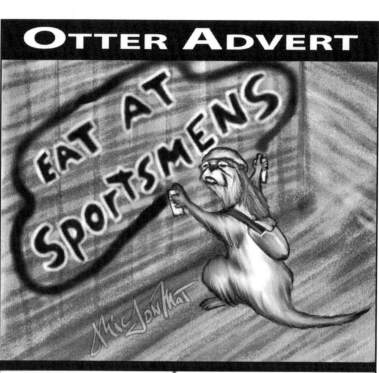

Other common forms are graffiti and baseballs, which were ideas that came from Earth. The graffiti is simple; just paint a message someplace a lot of people look and then run away really fast. The baseball thing is a little better. For that the otters write messages on balls and then throw them at random otters they come across. Then they run away.

The baseball message system is notorious for its efficiency. It's only natural to want to look at whatever just conked you on the head, and that's what most otters do. Of course, a lot of times the baseball misses, and breaks a window or something else, and then an otter is sure to pick up the baseball and save it because it broke a window.

That's how our advertising works, but I wasn't on Revir, and guessing things were going to be different on Earth, I suspected I would spend a lot of time being mad. I started immediately and began banging the glass window as another advertisement started. A flock of young humans was walking around in different places talking about some new product that helped alleviate the symptoms of something called herpes.

I continued to bang on the window and soon drew the attention of the human inside. He waved a hand at me and yelled for me to move on. I pointed at the TV, and then the Three Stooges returned.

I was glad to see my banging the window had produced a result. I watched another episode where the three men were playing the roles of doctors. By the time they completed an operation, leaving all the surgical tools inside the body, I was bent over in half trying not to throw up from sheer joy.

Then I heard another man's voice say, "The Three Stooges will be right back after these commercials."

So that's what they were called, commercials. I bristled at the new word and prepared to pound on the glass again, but I didn't. I decided that I could allow one commercial since it would allow me to recuperate myself and be better prepared to laugh. One commercial would be all right, but only one.

This advertisement had several dark-skin-toned humans talking. They all seemed to use the expression, "Wazzzup," throughout the commercial, and I found it amusing. I couldn't discern what was being advertised, but I didn't care.

Next came the Viagra commercial again, and I started pounding on the window. The man inside shook a fist at me, and I pointed at the TV. The Viagra commercial played on. I pounded some more and the man inside shook his fist again. I pointed at the TV. The Viagra commercial ended, and on came the herpes one.

Now I was mad, so I pounded harder. The man inside made a strange shape with his hand. His middle finger was pointing straight up while the rest of his fingers were clenched into a fist. Interpreting this as a hostile gesture, I shot him with my neural destabilizer so he fell to the floor unconscious.

Of course, that didn't solve the problem of the commercials, so I banged on the window some more.

Harassment

Someone shouted behind me, "Hey you!"

People seemed to use the word 'hey' a lot on Earth. I quit pounding on the window and turned around to see a man in uniform, the uniform of the human version of a rat. I tensed my muscles getting ready to pull out my PHESA.

Unsure what to say, I tried, "Wazzup?"

"What do you think you're doing there?" The Rat demanded before ordering, "Quit pounding on the window."

I relaxed my muscles. The rat didn't seem to be openly hostile. His manner was more that of a mother otter scolding an otterling.

"I'm trying to watch a program," I explained to him. "But these dirty commercials keep coming on."

The rat looked at me and shook his head. "Well, that's what happens when you watch TV. Go rent a video if you don't want commercials."

"Oh." The rat was even being helpful. "Where can I rent a video?"

"At a video store. What are you? Retarded?"

I ignored his tone and choice of words. "And then I can come here and watch it?"

"No, you dumb bum. You got a home?"

RAT WARNED

"Um...no."

"Well go get one."

"All right," I decided. "Where do I do that?"

The rat shook his head again. "You need a job first."

"A job?" I didn't like the sound of that. I thought I already had a job. "I have a job. I'm a bum."

"I can see that. Well a home's going to cost you 600 a month, then you'll need another 100 for a TV and player and then each video is about 15 bucks. Better start begging."

"Now wait," I told him, "600, 100, 15...are those dollars?"

"Yes."

I added up the numbers. "So for 715 dollars I can watch all the Three Stooges I want?"

"For a month maybe. Then it's another 600, plus food and everything else."

I scratched my head thinking. It took me nearly an hour to earn 5 dollars being a bum. To earn the first 715 I would have to work for 143 hours. Since there are 30 days in a month, I would have to work 4.8 hours a day, every day. Then there was the food. With all the laughing I expected to do watching the stooges, I anticipated requiring three fish a day, which I estimated would cost me at least 10 dollars a day. That would mean two extra hours of work every day.

So to watch the Three Stooges I would need to work almost 7 hours a day singing like a seal. I didn't think my voice could hold out that long.

I asked the rat, "How can I earn more money?"

"I dunno. Go to college. Get a better job."

"How long would that take?"

"Four years."

"That's too long."

"Of course, college will cost you."

"How much?"

"Depends. 5000 a year at the least."

"That's a lot of singing."

"What?"

"Never mind," I sighed with sadness. It felt like I was reliving a scolding from my mother, or reading one of the messages from the Pack. The effect was the same; don't do this, you should do this better, if you want to do this, do that.

That's the problem with the wolves. They're always telling us what to do. Whenever we have some fun they're always around to spoil it and tell us we're bad, and that reminds me. You won't believe this but collapsing stars really makes them mad. They use the stars to navigate in space and when we make the stars blow up they have to recalibrate their computers, which they don't like doing. Of course, that's the reason we collapse the stars, and whenever we can figure out a new good excuse for collapsing a star we do it.

And then there are the black holes. We used to have a program called, "Black Hole Collisions" and every week they'd crash a black hole into a planet or star or asteroid. That got the Pack mad too, but that's not surprising. They get mad about lots of things, even the planets. The last time they told us to build our own planets if we wanted to crash asteroids into them.

As far as I'm concerned the universe would be a lot more fun without the Pack, and talking to the human rat I was beginning to think that the money system used on Earth was something I could do without.

I just wanted to watch the stooges.

Revelation

After the painful discussion with the human rat, I retreated to the park and the bench, which was suddenly my only friend in the cruel, ugly, crappy world that I was stranded on.

Sitting there I thought through the events of the day and the lessons I had learned. Bleak is the word to describe the way I was feeling, having finally come to an understanding of the humans and their tortured existences. Billions of humans the world over were enduring some of the cruelest persecution in order to have money.

Money was the key to understanding the hairless monkeys. It was money and everything that money entailed. Money was needed to have shelter. Money was required to procure sustenance. Money was required to enjoy any luxuries available. In that last sentence is the demon, the key to the human's plight.

The humans worked for luxuries. To enjoy themselves they had to slave away. The greatest entertainment on Earth was within their reach, and yet to partake they had to prostitute their bodies. It was clear beyond a doubt that the humans were all suffering from an addiction to the Three Stooges.

It was sad, but somehow too real to be anything but what it was, which was, of course, sad.

To scratch my own Three Stooges itch I would have to actually become a human. A bum might be content with the low pay work that didn't involve actually working, but I assumed that was because they either hadn't been exposed to Moe, Larry, and Curly or that during their initiation rights they agreed to shun the stooges and their entire splendor in the pursuit of true spiritual liberty.

For me, it was too late. I'd seen the genius, and I could not ignore it. I was in the early phases of the addiction, so I could not yet be anything but excited about the stooges, but I'd spoken with several of the otters that made up the crew from the late 60's early 70's. It started that way, with the excitement, but then it progressed to bitterness. Each otter came to wish he or she had never started taking the drugs stolen from the long-haired humans, and quite possibly, some day I would feel the same way about the stooges.

It made sense and seemed to be the reason for the bitterness I was seeing everywhere in the human city. The humans were hooked on the stooges and had been hooked for years. The adults, in the advanced stage, could only work and keep satisfying the need but only because they couldn't live any other way, not because they found true enjoyment in it. The child humans on the other hand, as evidenced by their boisterous running about, were only in the early stages of addiction and still had a positive outlook on not only the stooges but also life itself.

I'd found a reason for living on Earth; to watch the Three Stooges, and yet I was no better off. Not only was I still lost and in danger of failing a mission, but I now also felt a need that I could not satisfy. Instead of being stranded outside in the rain, I was now stranded outside in a hailstorm.

Bleak is what I still was, but through every cloud a little sunlight must shine, and soon my powerful otter brain found two solutions to my problem. The first involved using the advanced Otternot technology at my disposal to achieve a more balanced distribution of resources between my human neighbors and myself, which we otters call theft. For that solution, I also needed a big stick to hit them on the head with after I zapped them with the neural destabilizer.

See, I'd noticed that nearly all the humans walking around were carrying money with them, and it seemed logical that one way to find employment would be to simply prey upon the humans who had jobs. It's called the 'stealing fish from your younger sibling idea' and it has a large following across the universe. One could almost call it mandatory for a healthy society because it's proven otter fact that once that predatory element isn't there in a culture the average citizen goes soft.

The other solution didn't sound as much fun as the first. It required completing my mission. If I completed the mission I could circumvent the entire process of money by simply getting Derbaron to find those comic geniuses the stooges and abduct them. I assumed this would be easy since the stooges were monochromatic and all the other humans I'd seen were polychromatic.

I vowed to go along with the shuttle when the abduction took place. I'm not supposed to talk about Derbaron's abduction record, but all the same, I'd never forgive myself if something like what happened to that Earhart woman happened to the stooges.

Otters tend to hold to abduction protocol as well as they hold to protocol in general and some more than others. For instance, the shuttles assigned to the Bermuda Triangle area have been under investigation for years because they keep coming home with their power supplies empty. We don't know exactly what they're up to out there, but we intend to find out.

Of course, our biggest problem area is botched abductions, which happen for all kinds of reason. Humans sometimes react badly to the bright lights shining in their faces. Some just stop and freeze like they're supposed to, but some panic and drive off the road and into trees or over cliffs.

Also, humans commonly take to discharging firearms at the lights, especially in the western areas of the United States and the poor areas of the big cities. When this happens the shuttle's computer automatically starts reducing the intelligence quotient of any nearby human, permanently. Then there are also the really fat humans that overload the engines on the shuttles. When that happens, the crew really has no choice but to jettison the cargo out of the largest spitter tube aiming for a lake or some other body of water.

There are also the humans that smell bad, which offends the shuttle computer, which then jettisons the human at some point between ground level and the upper atmosphere.

Basically; the whole abduction thing is a risky business. Mistakes are unmistakably destined to happen, but there'd probably be less if the pilots didn't all work for the government, which makes it difficult to fire them.

Friendship

As I was considering all these deep issues, a human dressed in a dark suit with a white shirt and black tie, sat down next to me on the bench. This was a new experience since most all the humans had avoided me as otters would an otter with a beaver tail. Curious as to the human's intentions, I chose to speak with the man.

I asked him, "Wazzup?"

The man smiled. "Not much buddy. How you doing?" I began to say something but was interrupted, "So, nice weather today for a change. Can't expect many more nice days out of this summer, but I suppose you know that better than me, eh?"

"Um… well-."

"Must move around a lot doing, well, you know. Yeah, must move around a lot. I know you can't stay here once winter creeps up. No, sir. You'd be dead before deer season…"

The human continued talking, but I was quickly losing interest. I assumed it didn't matter if I listened or not, since the man seemed to carry on the conversation without my interaction.

"You know what? I saw you from over there, and it really touched my heart. I had this uncle that lived on the street down in New Orleans or no wait that's what we all thought, but it turned out he had an apartment but got too plowed every night to get home. He just fell down and fell asleep wherever he felt like along the way. Funny, eh?"

"Um... yes."

"That's what I thought. I saw you from over there and I said to myself, now there's a guy that knows a joke when he hears one. I think it's those glasses of yours. That's hilarious. I like it, though. I mean, it really suits you."

"Um... thanks."

"Well, like I was saying, I fell off this cliff once – oh, wait, I didn't say that, did I? Oh yeah, well anyway, I was out with some buddies on the mine dumps up north. It was about midnight – you know – we were hitting the bottle, well anyway, I was right next to this cliff and all of a sudden there were all these bright lights and it just freaked me out."

"Hmm," I said uncomfortably, "That's unfortunate."

"Yep. Fell right off the cliff."

"That is unfortunate."

"Broke a leg."

"Hmm."

The human adjusted his tie. "You know what I was thinking when I woke up in the morning right next to the pit where I crawled out?"

"No-."

"I was thinking, gee, it'd sure be nice if someone was around to give me a helping hand, and you know, I think that's something important. A helping hand I mean, although two hands helping are better than one, but anyway when I saw you I thought to myself, gee, I bet that guy would really like a helping hand right about now. That'd be a good thing to do, to help another guy out."

"Um... yes-."

"I wanna give you a hand, friend. As a fellow creature of God, I think you deserve some attention, and I wanna help. What do you say? Could I buy you something to eat?"

"Um…" I thought about the offer. I was out of money, and I'd been sitting for some time thinking, and thinking is a very bad way to stay not hungry. I would need to eat again sometime in the future. I decided that it would be a good idea to accept, so I didn't. "No thank you."

"Why not? I don't mind. My apartment is just over there. See that building?" I looked where he was pointing and nodded. "It's right over there. You can have a late dinner with me, and we can talk about things. What do you say, pal?"

I thought about it again, but not very hard because I realized that the human had an apartment, which was what the human rat said I would need if I wanted to view the Three Stooges privately. To accomplish that there were other things needed, so I asked quickly, "Do you have possession of a TV and recordings of the Three Stooges?"

The man smiled. "A stooges fan, huh? Oh you bet, I must have twenty stooges' tapes." I nearly fainted from excitement. "We can watch a couple together. So you coming up, bud?"

"Yes."

With that, we made the journey to the building, where we used an elevator to get to the level where the human lived, and then went inside his apartment.

I was wary as I walked in because the room looked like the medical lab on the ship. The walls were all white and there was a table that looked to be for surgery in one corner. Elsewhere there were tools that looked to be used for cutting.

But then I spotted a soft looking bench in front of a TV, and I relaxed. Out of respect for my host, I waited as he entered and arranged his shoes and whatnot before I cut to the chase.

"Okay, let's start the stooges."

He pointed at the TV and said, "Knock yourself out."

Gleefully I darted to the TV and began rifling through the box containing the recordings. I quickly discovered that the human was indeed telling the truth. There were volumes of Three Stooges episodes and soon I was forced to decide which one I would watch first. It was a daunting decision.

"Yep, knock yourself out, buddy." I turned to inquire which episode was the worst so I could watch it first. That way it would only get better as I went along, but when I turned I saw that my host was holding a large club-like object over his head. "Actually, I'll knock you out."

And then he hit me with the club hard enough to make me see stars and knock me to the floor. The event was such a complete surprise that I froze with my eyes closed and by the time I broke free from the shock-induced paralysis, my host was crouched over me. I knew this without opening my eyes because I could hear him poorly imitating Curly, "Nuk nuk nuk. Why I outta." Then he laughed and shouted, "Paging Doctor Doc. C'mon in, Doc," he ordered, "It's all good."

Lying motionless on the floor I resisted the urge to look or ask what was happening while I heard a door open and a new male human voice ask, "What you mean paging? I don't got a pager. Nobody has a pager anymore."

"Forget it, Doc," my host giggled, "Let's just do this."

It was then I finally figured out that my host and his friend were trying to include me in some ritual of the human Three Stooges culture, possibly as a precursor to watching episodes.

Guessing the ritual was a reenactment of the Three Stooges episode I had seen where they played doctors, I then guessed that I was going to play a patient, which seemed logical since it was my first time inside the home and I was an outsider to the group who didn't know the ritual's details and therefore shouldn't be trusted with an important role in the performance, but thinking harder about the matter I wondered if I had been given a nonspeaking role due to my bum status, which also made sense because bums were exempt from work.

Curious which of the two was happening, I settled in to play my role as best I could and observe the human ritual as best I could without opening my eyes. When my host and Doc lifted me up I tried to be comically limp, and when they set me down I pretended to be dead to the world.

Then something poked my neck and I fell fast asleep.

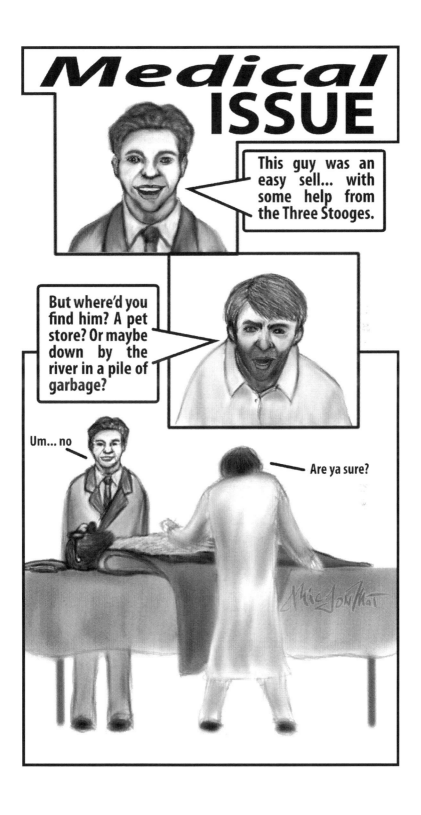

Surgery

When I awoke the two men were arguing.

"Just do it," my host was saying.

"I can't do it," Doc was telling my host. "I don't even think he's human. Look at him."

It was then I felt my bare fur was exposed to the open air. I remembered I was trying to play dead, but couldn't resist a quick glance. I saw my jacket had been opened and straps were pinning me to a long narrow table.

Glancing again I noticed Doc had a knife in his hand.

"I told you," Doc protested, "Whatever this thing is, it isn't human. If you want me to guess, it looks like some... kind of stretched out otter. Look, there's its tail, wrapped around it."

"Otters can't talk," argued my host.

"I know that," Doc said gesturing with the knife, "but that's what it looks like. It looks like an otter."

"And how would you know?"

"I am a vet. I'm supposed to know this stuff."

"I thought you were a real doctor."

"You don't need to be a doctor to take out a kidney."

"No," my host laughed, "Just if you want to do it right, but so wait... that means you should get paid less."

"We're not going to get paid," Doc complained, "cause this right here is not a human. There's no way it has a kidney. I'll prove it," he offered, "Here, just let me get through this fur."

Feeling fingertips pushing apart my fur I glanced down and saw Doc lowering his knife down to cut me and then my otter instincts kicked me into action. Deflating the air from my bones, I shriveled up to normal size, slipped out of my bindings and jumped to the far end of the table.

"Hey," my host commented, "it is an otter."

"I told you," the new man said.

Turning, I demanded, "This isn't a Three Stooges viewing ritual, is it?" Seeing the confused expressions on their faces, I was certain they had no idea what I was talking about, which meant everything was more or less exactly as it appeared and not at all as I had imagined.

Deeply disappointed, I groaned, "This is just a couple of monkeys trying to thief one of my organs!"

The men continued to stare at me with open mouths. Then Doc looked at my host and said, "It can talk."

With that, I went into a combat stance based on my training in Otter martial arts, which were founded after we discovered the beaver planet. Over 65 million years of study had gone into perfecting the style, and at that moment, I was about to display the techniques in their most developed form.

Otter open hand fighting technique, or Otkito, is probably the deadliest fighting system ever devised. The name means 'claw flying through the air impaling aggressor causing large amounts of pain' but that's just the basic technique. The more advanced forms and maneuvers sometimes have nothing to do with claws, or the teeth, although the best fighting works at the most basic level and an otter that has the basics down will beat a flashy otter that's clumsy.

Otkito is the art of synchronizing bone tendon air intake with movement to deliver maximum striking force at maximum range. Obviously, if you're going to hit something, the best thing to hit it with is something sharp, and that's where the claws come in, and as far as reach goes, pulling in air really fast into the tendons an otter can extend the length of a limb to five feet, and with that combination crippling blows can be delivered to any adversary.

That was the first thing I did, but I spiced it up a little. I spun 180 degrees and executed a spinning flying claw attack with my left foot. That made the attack less of a stab and more of a slash. I did this in order to strike both humans at the same time, which I succeeded in doing. The stunned humans fell away from the table and then having separated my enemies I took the opportunity to attack my host alone since he'd hit me previously and I'm vindictive.

In quick succession I delivered dozens of blows with the same extending of limbs, stretching arms and legs to strike with feet and fists. The attack wasn't a combination routine, just a flurry of hits aimed at exposed parts of his body, but I was following a rough strategy with my strikes.

OTKIDO JUSTICE

The name Otkido means 'claw flying through the air impaling aggressor causing large amounts of pain' but that's just the basic technique.

My goal was to hurt my host so bad and in such a short period of time that the pain overloaded his nervous system and caused his brain to black out.

Of course, I hadn't studied human anatomy enough to know if that was even possible, but at the time it seemed like a reasonable possibility and in any case, that's what I was trying to accomplish strategically during the beating.

After a few seconds, my host crumbled to his knees and then I delivered a final strike with my toes to his armpit, which caused him to collapse and have a bowel movement.

Then I turned to the would-be doctor, who was still holding the knife. To remove the knife I crouched low and then spun extending my tail. It was a tail whip attack, and it landed perfectly and disarmed the man.

Facing a single opponent I decided to show off. Pulling a lot of air into my limbs I inflated myself so I was seven feet tall and then chased Doc around the room intentionally hitting the walls near his head instead of hitting him so he could have enough time to properly appreciate the experience.

The whole time I was also pretending to be slower and less artful in my movements because when defeating an inferior opponent it's simple good sportsmanship to hide your skill so the over-matched opponent has a chance to hope for victory so that after the inevitable loss the opponent will be fooled into thinking the contest could have gone either way, which might lead to a rematch and a second easy win.

It was five minutes before I realized that I was probably never going to see Doc again, ruling out any possibility of him asking for a rematch. Then I tripped him with a tail sweep and systematically beat him with my fists until he looked remotely like an advertiser that got caught at an otter polo match.

Shrinking back down to normal size, I kicked Doc a couple more times to see if he moved, and then scurried over to my host and kicked him a few more times, just to be thorough.

Settled and safe, I gathered my disguise and prepared to make a quick getaway, as is natural for an otter after having caused destruction, but before leaving I went to the TV to steal the stooge recordings, and maybe to watch one before I left, since it would be a shame to waste such an opportunity.

Then I discovered I had been completely fooled. The boxes that claimed to contain the recordings were empty. Enraged I went back and kicked my host some more.

I knew that the extra kicking was excessive and ultimately about as pointless as calling a beaver ugly, but I couldn't help it. I had a right to be acting erratically. I'd nearly been cut open and had a vital organ removed.

In the heat of the moment, the trauma hadn't yet sunken into a feeling of violation, but I knew it would, which meant I should enjoy the anger while it lasted. I ripped the apartment apart, starting with the TV. Using Otkito I destroyed everything I could find. Then I went through the pockets of the two men, stole their money and made my way out.

Perhaps the deal on Earth is that instead of getting attacked by their computers, the humans just have accidents, and then they can't hate their computers for it cause they're so dumb it'd be like hating a rock; way too boring to hold your interest. I bet these monkeys don't even know how *real* hate feels.

Maybe I'm being paranoid and these things never break.

Nope. I called it right.

They break.

HELP

Looks like they break so often there's a built-in panic button.

You're telling me these things break so much the humans just gave up and adapted their designs to cope with chronic failure?

I was hoping that they broke so rarely it still hadn't happened yet

Why don't they rig one of the buttons to a bomb too?

That's not reassuring.

I'm...not sure I can do this.

Chapter 6

Gifted

I exited the apartment in a rush, retracing my way to the elevator, which I found to be confusing. There were a bunch of numbers in rows, and I'd press one and a light would come on, and I don't want to talk about it. I was starting to feel violated from almost having a kidney removed, and I panicked.

Running back into the apartment I tried to ask my former host how to use the elevator but that didn't work. The man was unconscious, but I did spy a staircase outside the apartment's window, so I made use of that instead and went out and down.

Arriving at ground level, as I had left the apartment in a rush, I was suddenly without my disguise of hat and glasses. I also had not taken the time to extend the fur around my face. So there I was, a man-sized otter dressed in a trench coat carrying a backpack.

Understandably the first person I saw reacted with alarm. The woman, standing beside her car, shrieked loudly, threw her belongings into the air and took off down the walkway, still screaming. The screaming was something I hadn't encountered in humans previously, and it shined a light on the ongoing research by Sinoperag, the head of Acoustic Amplification.

What Sinoperag does is research ways to produce and the effects of high-pitched-decibel sounds on humans. This all began after complaints from Derbaron after abducting female humans. He claimed they produced sounds alarmingly rich in both volume and pitch during the initial stage of the abduction or the 'prior-to-clubbing' phase as it is called.

Working off Derbaron's testimony, Sinoperag started running simulations to see the range of possible sounds a human female could produce, and came to the conclusion that the top end of some females voices was near limits fatal to small animals. The next step was logical: find a way to increase the range and sustainability of high-pitched-decibel sounds in the human female.

Collecting DNA from abducted female humans Sinoperag began his experiments to alter the female human characteristics to take advantage of the gender's natural inclination to scream shrilly and loudly. Initially, he had widespread success but when he requested permission to completely alter a female human for the purpose of sonic weaponry the Earth Security Department stepped in and held a hearing to test the pros and cons.

The Earth Security Department was worried that the humans could possibly use the sonic weaponry of their females to fight the otters if a war were ever to break out between us. On the other side of the issue, as always when something the Earth Security Department doesn't like is being discussed, was the Earthling Destruction Department, which wholeheartedly supported Sinoperag's idea and also war against humans in general.

They believed it was an ingenious method to finally weed out the human race from the planet's life forms, and their argument was simple. All humans began as child humans, and so all child humans had mothers or were exposed to females, and since they were smaller mammals than their adult counterparts, they would be more susceptible to the sonic weaponry of a female's voice. Since it was widely known that all female humans screamed from time to time, not only at their children but also their mates and more so the longer the couple was mated, it was assumed that in a short amount of time all the male and child humans would die off.

It was a debate that drew a large audience back on Revir. For the show just about every otter that was worth his tail showed up to testify as to what he knew about human behavior and tendencies, regarding the application of sonic weaponry.

That was before my time on the ship, but I'm sure that if I had been on the ship at that time I would've done exactly what my predecessor, Froidy, did. What Froidy did was to say he was above such a meaningless discussion and refused to get involved. By getting involved Froidy could've completely jeopardized the entire field of Human Psychology by showing that he didn't know anything.

Froidy knew better because he, just like I, had gone through the last year of training in Human Psychology, which has one lesson to teach: keeping your mouth shut. By the time graduation comes around we're all taught to speak for hours without really saying anything, and for our final examination we are required to do just that in a simulated press conference in which the professors ask questions as reporters normally would, and each graduate candidate is required to beaver flap his way through with flying colors.

Beaver flap is an interesting expression. It's stuck in our vocabulary even after the beaver wars because at the time of the wars it was commonly used. It's meant to refer to the stories the otters returning from the beaver planet would tell.

Since a single otter usually made the trip, there was usually a lack of witnesses to any fights that took place, and so the stories the trip fueled were always viewed with suspicion. Often the size of the beaver would increase with each retelling, along with the number of beavers and sometimes the number of teeth. The most famous beaver flap was a story about the time the otter Bunyan beat the snot out of a 30 ft tall, apparently mutated beaver named Babe.

So that's what beaver flap is, and in the Human Psychology department that's our pet name for the profession. We call our degrees 'diplomas of beaver flap' and our awards 'such and such award for beaver flapping beyond the call of duty'.

Anyway, my predecessor Froidy didn't try to beaver flap his way through the female human sonic weaponry debate, but he would've been right at home. The supposed experts disagreed for three days before the debate descended into an impromptu otter polo match, except instead of mallets they used random objects in the room and everyone was a striker.

When one of our debates breaks down that way, as about 64% of them do, we call it an 'Otterpoloo', and suspend the debate for 50 years, at which time all the experts will have gone back to Revir and new experts will testify. I'm looking forward to the next debate, which is only 21 years away. I plan on going just to watch and wait for the mayhem to start so I can get a crack at Mikey Fish.

This is a rather lengthy explanation, but being that I'm an otter I have a superior set of mental abilities, and so all this information went through my mind in the matter of a heartbeat. I noticed the use of sonic weaponry, found it annoying, wondered if Sinoperag had gone ahead with testing despite the Otterpoloo, and I picked up the woman's purse.

In it, I found more money and also the keys to the car that she had been standing beside. I thought about my need for transportation, and I got into the car, started it as I had seen Vel do, and then I began driving.

Slight Disorder

Driving can be a tricky thing when you're an otter. First of all the car was designed all wrong for my body configuration. Fortunately, I solved that by shrinking and expanding my body. Then I noticed mirrors in various spots throughout the car. These were meant to show areas behind the car while driving. I couldn't understand why that would be important, but intending to start my experiment correctly I shrunk and expanded again until all the mirrors served me usefully.

Then I tested the pedals underneath my feet. They didn't seem to do anything, although the one on the right seemed to increase the volume of the automobile's engine. I liked the increase in volume so I kept that pedal pressed to the floor.

Next, I tested some of the other controls, pondering their purpose. I spied something that looked like a computer in the middle of the car and I pressed a button just to test if it would allow me to use it. Immediately a voice came from speakers strategically hidden in the car. The voice explained that I should consult a doctor to see if Viagra was right for me, and I panicked again.

Pressing every possible button I succeeded only in increasing the volume of the rotten commercial. I was eventually forced to use my PHESA on the computer, an act strictly forbidden by otter law and something that I've always wanted to do. The voice stopped.

Happily I tried another control. This one was a stick

extending from the steering device, which moved a small arrow along a set of letters. Moving the arrow to the letter 'R' the car suddenly went backward.

By some stroke of luck, I slammed on the other pedal beneath my other foot and the car stopped. Pressing both pedals to the floor the sound of the engine rose again, but this time, I didn't like the sound. It was machine-like but wrong.

I didn't like going backward anyway, so I moved the stick again to the letter 'N'. I cautiously released the left pedal, which I will call the brake from here on out, but come to think of it I don't believe I ever used it again, and with the letter 'N' nothing happened. The car remained where it was, so I moved the arrow to the letter 'D' and suddenly I was driving.

I'm not sure how good my technique was. A lot of humans sounded horns, especially when I passed through intersections marked by strange signs reading 'Stop', but I wasn't sure if this was applause or irritation.

I wasn't too concerned anyway. I was enjoying the experiment, and I discovered that I was a natural automobile driver, maybe not in control or mastery of the humans' rules but I definitely had a flair for performing feats that the humans didn't dare to try.

I managed to never stop even though I didn't know where I was going. It wasn't difficult either as most of the humans were traveling at speeds 20 to 30 mph under the one I was going, and with such a difference and otter reflexes I simply used the maneuverable vehicle to twist out of stops.

I did this by making full use of my surroundings, which only seemed logical to me. On the wide roads, there were all kinds of space I could fit the car into with a minimum of scratching against the other automobiles. I also noticed that the oncoming traffic had a tendency to swerve off the road and crash when I drove in that lane.

This technique reminded me of a flight theory that Derbaron explained to me. According to Otternot flight rules, pilots are required to pass one another on the right when they are traveling in different directions. Of course, all flights are documented for the amount of time taken to fly from one point to another and back to the first point, and that's the only real system that exists for documenting pilot performance.

What Derbaron decided to do was increase his own marks, which he needed to do because he often hovered above drive-in movie theaters and dumped water on people in topless automobiles, and the way he chose to increase his marks was not by ceasing his fun and doing his job but by making all the other pilots look worse.

He did it by never passing on the right, but by firing an electrical blast and shooting the other shuttle out of the sky. Thanks to the self-detaching parachute and safety systems, no otters were hurt, and in a matter of minutes the computers on the shuttle would automatically reboot and the shuttle would resume its course.

Some of Derbaron's victims complained about the practice, which became known as the 'Derbaron hello', but Derbaron would always accuse the other pilot of firing first when he arrived back on the ship, and since the other pilot's computer had been shorted out by the blast, all his records had been wiped clean.

Intelligently the other pilots quit complaining and started fighting back. Before long any two shuttles that passed each other out of sight of the main ship were firing at one another. Derbaron, since he is now the head of the pilots, obviously was the winner of most of the air battles.

And I liked his strategy. At one point a loud siren went off and I noticed flashing lights behind me. I saw this in the mirror, and I didn't turn around to look because I was performing a complicated maneuver weaving in-between two parked automobiles, jumping my automobile onto the curb of the walkway and aiming for a blue box.

At that point, I turned and fired my neural destabilizer at the car with the flashing lights, because it was annoying, and it proceeded to crash into something. I quit looking back and set my sights on the blue box.

I wasn't sure of the purpose of the blue box, but I found out later that it was used to store letters sent from one human to another. If I had known that, and that the box was made of a very solid metal, I wouldn't have attacked it with my car.

But not knowing that, I did attack it with my car, and soon the glass before me was shattered and the mailbox was wedged halfway inside my car where a passenger would normally be seated. Letters flew out from the box as I swerved back onto the street and toward an intersection with a red light baring my advancement.

I was forced to slow down because dozens of cars were crossing the intersection in front of me, but very quickly I spotted a gap in the cars and then I ignored the danger and went through the red light. The applause was thunderous.

The reason I attacked the blue box was because it reminded me of a traumatic episode from my childhood. I was born after the beaver wars, and I grew up after the rats were being phased out, but unfortunately the otter rulers had gotten used to having the general population under some kind of control, and so they instituted the Random Punishment System.

The system worked under the assumption that all otters broke the law. No one argued the validity of this assumption, but they did argue the next one, which was that all otters should be punished for breaking the law.

To punish all otters for breaking the law, the rulers set up blue boxes in various areas throughout the otter cities, and then established quotas based on the local crime rate.

However many laws were broken during a month, the next month that same number of punishments would be randomly distributed throughout Revir.

The blue box, randomly as an otter passed, would spray out a load of blue sludge, staining the otter's fur for the next month, which caused that otter to be teased by everyone that came across him, and hence the punishment.

I myself was a victim of this punishment. It was in my early days, and I personally made use of the blue boxes for a game of chance I called 'test your fate'. The game was a simple experiment to better understand how the punishment system randomly chose victims, or that was what I told my friends after I dared them to run by the blue box hoping they would get splattered blue.

OTTER RIDE

OESG Note on Cars:

Experts believe the principle purpose of cars in human society revolves around mating, with prospective mates using the style of driving, choice of music and the car's model to evaluate its driver.

The latest research concludes the most favored automobiles are those with high insurance premiums, top speeds and carrying capacity, signifying a mate capable of bulk purchasing and fetching.

Unfortunately after three months, during which time they'd all been blue at one point or another, they tied me to a pole in front of the blue box where I was sprayed a total of 11 times during a period of two days, after which my mother noticed I was missing and set me free.

Attacking the blue box was a reflex reaction. I had a score to settle, and in hindsight, it was worth it, since I survived.

Personal War of Malice

My tale took a bad turn as I was messing with more of the buttons. Somehow I had touched something that was causing the inside of the car to overheat, and try as I might I was unsuccessful in restoring the former climate. Also, the shattered window made it difficult to see. I was forced to fly by instrument, as Derbaron would say. This was difficult since there were no instruments in the automobile to show my position or the position of the cars around me.

This was troubling because I was very much enjoying the experience of driving. But as with all good fun, there is a point at which it becomes dangerous. My otter reflexes and mental capabilities could only do so much, and if I couldn't figure out a way to see where I was going I was destined to force the automobile into a bouncing situation with another solid object.

Hitting one such object the automobile spun out of my control and I began spinning in circles, scattering whatever it was that used to be where I was spinning in circles.

When the spinning stopped, I was dizzy. Opening the car door to spit up the fish I had eaten that afternoon, I found I was again in the park. For some reason, I had come full circle.

I had been free flowing with my choice of direction while driving, so ending up at the park must have been the result of some unknown subconscious desire. I sat in the night air and thought about why I would want to come back to the park.

Then I spotted it, staring at me unmistakably. The electronic store with the TV's on display through the window was not far off, and I knew what had happened.

I was returning to the stooges. I was hopelessly hooked on the drug, and I came fully to the realization that my life would be forever changed thanks to those three humans. No longer would I enjoy the simple pleasures of life. I would be forever thinking about what I could be doing, about how much I could be enjoying the complicated and fulfilling entertainment of those three masters.

My life was in shambles, so to speak. I was out of control, living only to satisfy a need that I did not have yesterday.

I was on a mission and not a human. I shouldn't have a need for the drug that forced the humans to lead busy lives and sell their souls.

"I am an otter," I said resolutely, knowing what I needed but not yet know knowing how to go about getting it. I thought for a moment. Closure was needed. My addiction had to end and to end it I had to destroy the trigger that started it. To suit my personal interests, I decided the electronic store would have to die.

I was sure it was the source of my problems, just as every otter that grows up cross-eyed knows it was because of his or her older sibling or siblings. In their developing stages otterlings have a fascination with purple objects, and if such a purple object is placed in front of him or her, the otterling will stare at it for however long the purple object is there.

Older otterlings know this and amuse themselves by placing the purple object on the tip of the youngest otterlings' nose, causing the younger otterling, after only 23 hours of this, to become cross-eyed. For such an otter, growing up is difficult until it reaches maturity and can undergo corrective surgery. For such otters, in the first few moments of seeing the world clearly, their first action parallels the one I was about to undertake.

Those newly uncross-eyed otters beat the beaver flap out of their older siblings because they caused all the problems, and I was about to beat the beaver flap out of the electronics store.

Getting the automobile to smash into it would be tricky. On either side of the store windows were solid brick areas of the building. Crashing into either of those spots was risky.

I needed to see where I was going. Then I spied the letter 'R', and the rest came naturally. Driving backward into the electronics store with a mailbox protruding from my car, I prepared to execute a blowfish maneuver.

I assumed that the collision would be dramatic and exciting, and living through such experiences is the mantra of the blowfish maneuver, but upon colliding with the store, I discovered that the humans had discovered this as well. In the midst of shattering glass, bending plastic and electric shocks, two bags of air exploded from the middle of the steering device and from the area in front of the passenger seat.

The bag of air dislodged the mailbox and projected it into a previously untouched TV. The bag of air striking me had worse results. I was in the middle of a blowfish maneuver, and that is a sensitive time. My air values were all open letting in air, and so there was also the possibility of air flowing out.

The two impacting objects filling with air resulted in one of them expelling its air. The sound of this happening, of an otter getting all the air squished out, is roughly similar to an elephant farting, and in the electronics store, it caused everything made of glass that wasn't already broken, to shatter.

Now normal sized I struggled to free myself from the automobile. An alarm was sounding and I knew it'd only be a matter of time before human rats showed up to investigate. Eventually, I was forced to bite my way out. I left the remnants of my disguise in the car and shuffled out of the store. Along the way, I saw a copy of a Three Stooge's episode. Realizing I shouldn't pick it up, I picked it up.

Sterile Voices

After the crash, I ambled along thinking about my situation. Normally I would've completely ignored it, as per otter instinct, but I decided that ignoring was no longer an option. I was stuck and needed to be unstuck for my life to continue effectually. Lost in the world of humans, I thought through the matter and decided that in order to navigate my way I would have to accustom myself to humans, research their habits, learn their primitive technologies and integrate into their lifestyle.

151

Resolving problems through destructive acts is often unwise but usually this is only in retrospect, leaving any present minded otter free to enjoy its many short-term therapeutic effects repeatedly.

OTTER CLOSURE

I feel... *good* about this.

I didn't like that idea so I searched for a way to cheat. As far as cheating went, I knew that for proper cheating the main requirement was an extensive knowledge of the system to be cheated, but then that led back to my first idea about all that hard work and learning. But there was another option.

I didn't have to exactly learn everything about the humans. I could simply find a human and learn only what was necessary to accomplish my mission. Of course, that left me with another problem. The problem was I didn't know any human that I trusted to help me cheat.

I didn't know the names of many humans at all. The only human I did know was Percivel Tyse, a young male human from the city of Hibbing in the north of this section of the world called Minnesota, the same young male human that had alleged otters were related to muskrats.

He'd also pushed me out of his automobile at a speed of 70 mph, as I first recalled it, but thinking about Vel, I had to admit that given the limitations of the average human, mistaking an otter for a muskrat wasn't such an unforgivable sin. The ignorant couldn't help being ignorant, and he hadn't actually pushed me out of his automobile. He had only infuriated me into exiting out of my own free will.

I thought that perhaps there was hope for that young male human, but I anticipated problems trying to contact him. I decided, against better judgment, to look in the OESG. I perused the pages for almost an hour as I sat, cloaked, on a bench in the park. I eventually found something useful within all the beaver flap under 'alternative uses for human coins':

Humans use payphones, which are devices used to communicate between two humans that happen to be holding a phone to his or her ear. A great way to amuse oneself is to dial random numbers and talk to the person that answers.

I thought about trying that, but before I could I had read the next section:

If you are searching for a specific human, for abduction or other purposes, simply press the '0' button on the phone and a human will instruct you as to which number combination will provide access to that particular person.

Note - Rulers and bums are difficult to reach this way.

Suddenly filled with information I threw the OESG back into my pack and started to walk. It seemed to me, as with everything else, the humans had their own special way of doing things. We otters have the capability to use such a system as the human phones for communication, but most of us can't use it because the computers won't let us, and being that we are stuck with the stupid machines we rely almost completely on the old system of writing letters.

A computer might be nice and helpful to a small portion of the otter population, but that niceness does not extend to jobs initiated by a computer privileged otter that doesn't directly affect that specific otter. For instance, if we were to transmit messages using the computers, the only messages that would get through would be the messages sent by and to otters that the computers like. All other mail would probably come garbled or horribly altered if it came at all, and regular paper letters aren't safe either. The rotten computers that control the ships that deliver mail between the planets are constantly trying to open up airlocks to blow all the mail into outer space, or trick the crews into burning the mail with false ship alarms and the occasional threat if they're really ticked off.

It's a tricky thing living with a machine that hates you, but there's something to say for being kept on your toes, and I was confident I could handle the human system. I hadn't gone far when I discovered a payphone located inside the park. I picked up the earpiece, and punched the number '0'.

I was put on hold, or so I was told by the sterile-sounding voice on the phone. After a moment, the phone clicked and a woman's voice greeted me, asking what services I required.

"I would like to talk to Percivel Tyse."

"And where does Mr. Tyse live?"

"The city of Hibbing, in the north of this section of the world called Minnesota."

"All right, one moment please." After a short pause, her voice came on again. "I have a number for a Luke and Jennifer Tyse, but no Percivel is listed. Would you like that number?"

"Sure."

"Thank you for calling." The operator's voice clicked off and a sterile sounding voice came on.

"The number you wish to dial is, area code 218-555-2893. Thank you for calling."

The phone clicked and I heard the same droning beep as when I first picked the phone up. I looked quizzically at the numbers and began hitting them. Another sterile voice said I needed to dial 1 first.

Family Interference

After braving the line of sterile voices, I heard a ringing. I waited and heard another ringing. I waited and heard another ringing. Then a voice, human and female, began talking.

"Hello." The greeting was short.

My reply was short. "Wazzup?"

"Um...can I help you?"

"Could I speak to Percivel Tyse?"

"Vel isn't here. He's back down in the cities."

"Where is he in the cities?"

"Inver Grove Heights."

"All right...where am I in the cities?"

"Um...I don't know."

We were having communication problems I blamed on the gender divide, so I tried to start over, "I need to talk to Vel."

"I could give you his cell phone number."

"What's a cell phone?"

With a confused voice, the female asked, "What?"

"Never mind."

We were continuing to have problems.

"I was saying, I could give you his cell phone, but he doesn't want us to give it out. Are you a friend of his?"

"No, not really. He threw me out of his car."

Again confused, she asked again, "What?"

"Never mind. I would like the number for his cell phone."

"Um," I sensed hesitation in the female human's voice. "Who are you?"

"My name is Spock. Who are you?"

"Spock? That's funny. I'm Ashley."

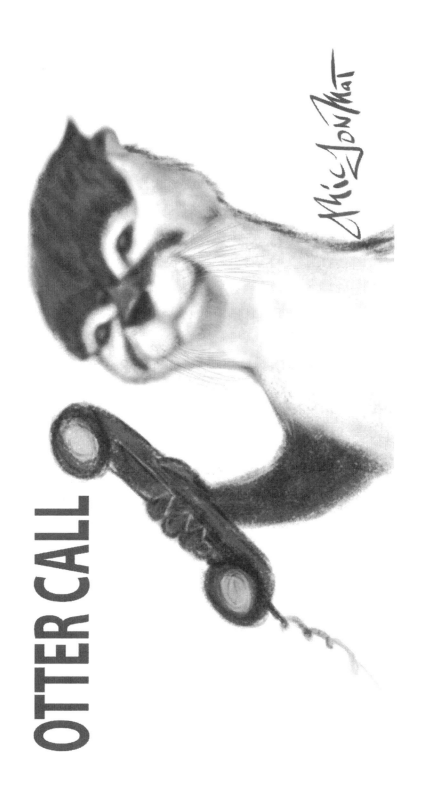

OTTER CALL

"Ashley? That means...never mind." I was about to tell the female that her name meant muddy water in my language, but knowing female otters, I didn't.

"Spock. Hmm. Maybe I could call Vel and ask him if it's all right. Do you have a number I could call you back on?"

"I'm at a payphone."

"Well, what's the number on it? Does it have one?"

I examined the payphone and discovered a marking that I assumed must be a number of some kind. "Yo mama."

"My... my what? Is that supposed to be a joke?"

"Oh wait, here's some numbers." I read the girl the numbers and she told me Vel would call me if he wanted. I told her she was at least a competent secretary. She told me she was Vel's sister, not his secretary, and then hung up without a goodbye.

The difficulties I'd experienced made sense after hearing she was Vel's sister. Any otter can appreciate the difficulties presented by siblings, in early life and beyond. Most of our tragedy plays, three of the four of them, are based on siblings fighting and eventually killing one another. Brothers and sisters, we've discovered, are better raised in teams of just brothers or just sisters. Most males that grow up with a sister of nearly equal age usually end up living solitary lives because they've already been exposed to evil female tendencies.

I was raised as an only otter, but I had female cousins and during family gatherings when the adults were absent, they usually tortured me, which is something I refuse to go into details about, but my cousins were only cousins and growing up I simply assumed they were insane, so I didn't come to have a prejudiced opinion of female otters in general.

Agreement

I waited for some time near the payphone. I was reliving in my mind some of the slanderous accusations of Vel. His range of blasphemy was wide and varied from the otter's actions toward the humans to the otter's actions toward the dinosaurs. Basically, he'd objected to everything that was otter, and he'd called us cousins to the beavers.

The mistake the citizens of Atlantis made was similar to

Vel's, but while the Atlanteans were stupid, Vel had been exposed to the wisdom of otter reasoning and then rejected it. Not only had he rejected it, he'd soiled it with words as harsh as ever spoken by a beaver and I didn't anticipate he'd changed his attitude since my exiting his automobile. Thinking about it harder, the way I exited his automobile might have inadvertently supported his view of the otters.

It was typical. No matter what, when I'm in trouble it seems the only way to get out of it is to undergo some type of torture, such as the visits to my uncle's house. The only way to get away from the adults who forced me to sing was to play with my cousins that would... never mind what they did, and on the ship, it was the same thing. No otter I have a problem with is going to care unless a physical confrontation occurs, or if someone higher up tells them to be nice, and since I'm a department head the only place I can go is to the Man, and I don't like the Man.

The Man had gotten me into this trouble, and now I was hoping to get out of it by seeking the help of Vel, someone superbly gifted in annoying me. Thinking of the ways he could annoy me, it immediately occurred to me that the best way would be to just not call.

Then the phone rang. I picked it up.

"Hello?"

Vel's voice asked, "Is that you, Kirk?"

"No. This is – wait – you know exactly who this is."

"Sure I know. It's... kinda nice to hear you're alive, I guess."

"No thanks to you."

"Oh yeah, about that, why'd you tell my sister I pushed you outta the car? I didn't push you. I didn't even touch you."

"You willed me to jump out. Don't deny it."

"Fine," Vel sighed, "Truce. What do you want?"

"I need your assistance in finding the Como Zoo."

"What happened? You're at a payphone in Minneapolis."

Unsure what that had to do with anything, I asked, "So?"

"So... I don't know," he giggled for some reason, "That's a long way from where you jumped outta my car."

"I used other means to travel."

"What? You mean besides carjacking?"

"It's a long story," I replied, "that I'm trying to forget."

"Fair enough. So what do you want?"

"I want to go to the Como Zoo."

"It's too late tonight. The zoo's closed."

"I don't care."

"So what do you want from me?"

"I need transportation."

"Oh yeah? And what's an inferior human like me supposed to do about that with my... tiny inefficient brain?"

"You have an automobile," I explained, "and you can drive, and in exchange for your help I will give my word that I won't have you abducted when I get back to my ship."

"Oh, we're making a deal. Alright," Vel accepted, "I bet I could just let you rot and I wouldn't have to worry about it anyway, but alright. I'll help you out for the karma points."

"Good, be quick-."

"But first, you gotta say you wish you were a beaver."

As the words sank in, I bared my teeth. "Say what?"

"You heard me. I wanna hear you say you wish you were a beaver. Make a rhyme out of it, like, 'a beaver is what I'd like to be because beavers are so much smarter than me.'"

I cringed and shivered at the idea. "You're kidding."

"No, I'm serious," Vel pressed, "Say it and then I'll help."

Shaking a clenched fist at the phone I refused, "Never!"

"You got ten seconds to say it," Vel warned, "or I'll think up something even worse to make you say."

Over the course of those ten seconds, I spat on the ground, pulled out some of my fur, chewed my whiskers, ran my claws down my face, kicked a garbage can close enough to the payphone to hit with a stretch, and then I swallowed my pride and choked out the terribly bitter words.

Chapter 7

Awaiting Debating

After I had been forced to blaspheme against my own species, I was then forced to wait for the human named Vel. He had me walk to the nearest intersection and read the names of the signs and then report back to him. Somehow by the markings on the signs, he was able to tell where I was.

As an otter, I couldn't understand this system since we've always thought it was tacky to put labels on locations. It insinuates the otter reading the sign doesn't know where he or she is in the first place and is therefore tacky. Also, it is a form of advertisement, which as I explained is banned throughout the otter worlds.

In contrast, the signs we do allow to be placed in various areas are meant to serve useful purposes, like distracting otters from ugly things, like new construction sites and any areas where explosions recently took place. The way it works is simple. A snapshot of a very good otter polo hit is posted in the direction away from the ugly spot, and more otters than not will admire the sign instead of the ugliness.

Vel didn't care about any of that. He said he now knew where I was, and he'd be over as soon as he could.

"See you, Kirk."

"My name is-," and the phone went dead.

I slammed the phone down and walked back into the park. My mind was heavy with thoughts, so I did my best to ignore the situation by returning to the other side of the park where I'd crashed the car into the electronics store. As usual, the humans seemed to be in a hurry to make things the way they were. A special vehicle was being used to extract the automobile from the store and a throng of human rats was gathering information, paying special attention to my discarded disguise and the mailbox. There was a strange looking rat with 'FBI' written on his jacket looking over the mailbox. He seemed to be laughing.

I climbed again into the tree that I had first occupied in the park and watched the biped tail-lacking beavers at work. In such a situation, my mind seemed unable to resist wondering what life was trying to teach me.

We otters have a proverb that deals with the situation I was in, "Worlds and words are dirty and wise is the otter who knows where the water is to wash them off."

I say that proverb applied to my situation because no otter has ever figured out exactly what it means, and therefore we try to apply it to every situation. The way I was trying to apply it was that currently, I was getting dirt thrown on me by life, which was the life dictated by the human world, and I needed to find some water to wash away the dirt. I needed to get back to my otter self in order to be rightly balanced in my place in the universe.

What the dirt was, specifically, was the human culture. I had too quickly assumed the humans were simple and stupid, and I'd been sucked in by their cleverest trick, the stooges. What I should have assumed was that the humans were complicated and stupid. That would have made me more cautious, and I wouldn't have experienced the culture shock of the full immersion into human society.

I also could've taken the time to better read the OESG's section on human society. It had been compiled based on interviews with hundreds of human abductees and therefore likely held a glimpse into the utter confusion of human life. Having lived that life, I didn't feel like reading about it. Instead, I felt a better use of time would be to complain about everything I'd seen, and to use my experiences to validate the basic principle of Human Psychology.

That basic principle is that humans are nuts, and one human I was sure was nuts was Vel.

I'd given my word that I wouldn't have him abducted, and it is the second foremost rule of otter honor, the second foremost of the two of them, that once given an otter's word be kept at all cost. But the foremost rule is that an otter shall not blaspheme by speaking any words that could be interpreted as acknowledging that the beavers are intelligent.

Vel had forced me to break the foremost rule, and so the second rule, in my mind, no longer mattered. I'd never heard of the complication arising so there wasn't a hard set precedent, but it was logical. After committing a class six violation it didn't make sense to have reservations about committing a class five, so I planned on having Vel abducted, and I'd make sure he ate the banana, which is important.

Upon first hearing of it, the banana may seem unnecessary because it's basically just a banana. But understanding Human Psychology, understanding that humans are nuts, the banana takes on a different meaning. The human naturally believes it is a consumer, and not just a consumer, but also the top consumer. A human sees the world as functioning only to serve the consumption of the human species, and other larger animals physically superior to the humans have been hunted, killed and subjugated in order to forward this myth of humans on top of the food chain.

Now the banana is a simple object. It doesn't move and it can't defend itself, and so when a human bites a banana and finds that the banana has grown back despite the bite, the whole thought structure of the human is effectively collapsed. No longer is the human the top of the food chain, controlling all and master because a simple dumb banana is frustrating the human's best efforts at consuming it.

Most humans, when this thought structure collapses, have characteristically insane reactions. A smart and publicly conscious organism would do its utmost to steal the banana in order to supply the world with an inexhaustible food source, but not a human. Most humans throw the banana at the wall farthest away, or they break down and laugh like lunatics.

We otters prefer the ones that laugh. They seem to be better able to adapt to the shock, and if there's any hope for the humans it's through such lunatics. Unfortunately, like honest otter rulers and mild-tempered weasels, these lunatic humans are rare. Initially in the late 60's and early 70's we had high expectations of the humans because they seemed entranced by the growing banana and asked if they could keep it, but then we discovered that they were just on drugs.

Hostile Escort

It took almost an hour for the soon to be abducted human to arrive. When he did his attention went magnetically toward the scene at the electronics store with all the rats. While he was distracted I sneaked into his automobile.

When I shut the door he began driving the car again. I turned off my cloaking device.

"Nice night," he commented. I did not reply. "That wasn't your doing back there was it?" I did not reply. "Lot's of stuff happening today. A news helicopter crashed, there was a bunch of car accidents, and then there was that thing over there. I heard something about it. Something about a mailbox, I don't really remember." I did not reply. "News said the woman whose car it was said she had it stolen by a monster or a criminal in a mask." I did not reply. "She said he looked like a giant beaver."

I glared at the human and prepared to execute a jabbing double right claw extension eye gouge of fury, which I had invented after watching the stooges. It would have placed two of my claws into Vel's eyes and likely caused blindness.

"I don't like you," I said instead.

"So that was you causing all this mayhem. I should report you to somebody."

"I should destroy you."

Undeterred, Vel continued to annoy me. "Ever thought about working for a circus? You'd make a good freak."

I took a deep breath to calm myself. Vel would eat the banana I told myself, he would eat the banana until he forgot what everything tasted like besides the banana.

"Did you have fun anyway?"

"Oh, bunches," I finally spoke. "One of you hairless monkeys tried to steal my kidney."

Vel frowned. "You're kidding? What, were you dressed like a bum or something?"

"Yes."

"Oh, well you should report them." Vel eased back in his seat and his head began to bob up and down. I got the impression he was thinking. "So you dressed up like a bum? But you're kinda short. Can you change shape at all?"

I nodded.

"That's cool. So you can make yourself human size?"

I nodded.

"Huh. You know, that wasn't a bad idea. I bet people couldn't even tell if you wore a hat or something. Just make it look like you had a beard. Yeah, that would work."

I shrugged. "It worked until the kidney thing."

"It was still working then, though. When did they figure out you were a freak?"

I hissed softly, but I didn't feel as if the human meant to offend me. Instead, I had the impression he was trying to joke. "I was on a table. They were about to cut me open."

"What'd you do then? Did you use that zap gun of yours?"

I was suddenly reminded that my disarmed matter destabilizer was still in my possession, and set to self-destruct at some point in the next 86 days. "No, I used Otkito, our style of fighting."

"Otkito," Vel repeated chuckling, "That's awesome. So you beat them up, huh?"

"Yes." After that, there was a pause in the conversation as Vel made some complicated turns onto one of the major roads, which required his full attention.

"So how did they grab you?" He asked as his attention returned to me.

"Grab me?"

"Yeah, how'd they get you to where they could cut you open?"

"Oh." I grimaced at the memory. "I was lured to their apartment. They promised to let me watch the Three Stooges."

Vel nodded. "You know about them, huh?"

"Oh yes," I said grimly, "I know all about the Three Stooges."

Vel tapped his steering device. "That's good stuff."

"Oh yes," I agreed, "Too good."

"Yep," Vel said with a smile and sigh I assumed were signs of his addiction, "You can't beat the three wise men."

PERCIVEL TRUCE

"Ah, I see you are addicted too. It's been a few hours now for me. How many recordings do you watch nightly?"

"Um, none. I used to watch them when I was a kid. I don't know. I should get some."

I stared at him to see a sign that the overgrown loopey was lying. "You mean, you don't watch them regularly?"

"No. I don't watch much TV."

"Why not?"

"I don't have one."

I stared at him for a long moment. I wasn't sure if my previous logic, that all humans were addicted to the Three Stooges, was flawed, or if Vel, as unusual as I found him, was also unusual as far as humans went. Either I had been wrong and here was a normal human, or I was right and here was an exception human. I decided upon the latter since it seemed more likely that I had found one freak human than I had been wrong.

I asked, "So, you don't watch the stooges every night?"

"No, but I've probably seen all the episodes."

I decided that I had found a freak human, and I was sure that when Vel ate the banana he would laugh at it. I had found Vel's saving trait.

Saving traits are important. Back when the Pack stopped the war, many of them held the opinion that we otters were a menace that the universe was better off without. These simple-minded wolves wanted to blow up our planet, but in typical wolf fashion, they had to reason it out beforehand.

What they did was to make us present our cultural achievements to see if we were adding anything to the benefit of intelligent life forms in the universe. We couldn't think of anything to show them, so they came to Revir and took in the sights.

They watched several otter polo matches, which they didn't seem to understand, and then they listened to some dolphin and wolf music, but that didn't count because it came from other worlds. Then there was Otkito, but that was a destructive fighting technique that wasn't applicable for other species, and then there were our four tragic plays, various documentaries we'd done, our computer systems, which really annoyed the wolves, and our justice and advertising systems.

After a year of cataloging otter society, they were about to submit their report to the Pack counsel, advising the council to seriously consider genocide. Then to celebrate the completion of their assignment, and their upcoming parting from what they described as 'the most insane planet in the universe', they asked to dine at our most expensive restaurant.

The restaurant was home to Revir's best fish fryers, and they were world renowned for their ingenious recipes. They waved the slapping admission and refrained from spiking the wolves' food. The wolves ate over 400 slaps worth of food and then rewrote their report to the council, this time advising the council to deal diplomatically with us otters.

What the wolves had discovered was our saving trait. That trait was the ability of our cooks to make fish taste like anything.

"Like anything?" Vel asked after I had explained this.

"Yes. And that saved our planet."

"What about chocolate? Can they make fish taste like chocolate?"

I nodded and laughed, "Otterling's play."

"What about rice? Can they make it take like rice?"

"Yes," I confirmed, "but they'd be beaten for it."

"What about coffee. Coffee flavored fish?"

"Commonly eaten by office working otters or offotts."

"Bacon?"

I shrugged. "I don't know what the beaver bacon is."

"Strawberries?"

"One of the most popular flavors."

"Lemons? Licorice? Bat? Baboon? Gerbil?"

Parting of the Non Enemies

"You sure about this? I can take you to the zoo tomorrow."

"No," I told Vel, "I'd rather sleep outside. After five years in a spaceship, I forgot how much nicer planets are."

After discovering the common bond of the Three Stooges, Vel and I had gotten along well. It was unparalleled in history that an otter and a sober human parted as friends, so I wanted to be the first to do so.

To do this I had him explain to me a public system of transport known as the bus. He was to leave me at one such place, where I would sleep, and in the morning I would take the proper bus to the Como Zoo and complete my mission.

Vel had offered several times to let me sleep at his house, and even tempted me by promising to illegally obtain stooge videos by a process called downloading, but I remained firm in my resolve to associate as little as possible with him in order to maintain the balance we had discovered. It was my belief that prolonged association would undoubtedly lead to problems and likely a resumption of hostilities.

"Well," he said almost sadly, "I guess you're ready."

He'd just finished explaining to me the bus system, instructing me how to properly use it so that I didn't find myself many miles from my intended location.

"Yes. I suppose that is it. I thank you for your services. I repeat that I will not have you abducted when I return to the ship."

"Okay. Those bananas sound pretty interesting, though."

"Well, never mind."

There was an awkward pause, and then I instituted the otter method of saying goodbye. Normally, when we plan on seeing the other otter again soon, we don't say goodbye, but when an extended period of time might take place, we use a special method. It begins with a staring match. I began to stare at Vel. He stared back. He asked, "Why are we staring at each other?"

I told him, "This is how we otters say farewell."

"Okay," he nodded, "I'll just... keep staring at you then."

We stared for almost two minutes and then I looked away. Two minutes is pretty good time for a stare down, so I wasn't too upset with it.

I told Vel, "You win."

"Good," he said with a shrug, "So what now?"

"Now you bite my tail."

I turned around to provide access to my tail. Vel laughed, "Bite your tail?"

"Yes. You won the staring contest so now you bite my tail."

He shook his head, "I'm not gonna bite your dirty tail."

"Just bite it. That is how we say farewell on Revir."

"Yeah... but.... we're not on Revir, so," he laughed, "this is how we say goodbye on Earth, Dr. Jones."

"My name is-," and then he kicked me in the butt.

Public Transport

During the night, I refreshed myself by letting my mind go completely blank. This is typical for otters during sleep, but somehow, also typical, is a feeling of extreme depression in the morning when it becomes all too clear that there will be no more peace until the next journey into sleep.

This was made clear by the torrential downpour that erupted while I was peacefully asleep. The storm was marked with a bunch of lightning, thunder and of course lots of falling rain. It was instantly upon me, and I had no chance to get under cover or to even cover up my open survival kit, which I had pulled over my head to keep out any noise.

I was in a field near the bus stop, and when the commotion broke out I made haste to get to the bus stop shelter. In my haste, I forgot my survival kit, but I didn't realize I'd forgotten it until a bolt of lightning struck the field were I was, and effectively obliterated all of my otter belongings, and yes, sadly, my Three Stooges recording.

Stripped of all my superior technology, except for my personal cloaking device and PHESA, I tried to go back to sleep. I failed and instead shivered as the storm pounded away all around me, until the violent weather passed. Then I shivered as the sky cleared and the stars came out. Then the sun came out and began to dry the land. Then the bus came.

Needless to say, I was not in the best of moods as I climbed aboard the bus and hid underneath a chair. From my lowly place, I could hear the moving about of several child humans in the bus and the scolding of their mothers. I found it interesting for about 20 seconds, and then I climbed up to where I could get a better view of the land we were passing through.

I sat, still shivering in one of the seats next to the window and tried to screen out the various sounds of humanity around me. It was too early in a day too crappy to put up with human idiocy. I had exceeded my tolerance limit.

I made ready my PHESA in case any of the children came too close. but they not did, initially, so I was refused one of the most basic forms of otter therapy. There are various types of otter therapy, ranging from mental to physical to emotional to reproductive. Each field, although bearing a different name is just an alteration of basic therapy. Basic therapy is available only to otters that have undergone a traumatic experience, such as being near one of the many accidental explosions that occur on Revir, or parents after the birth of an otterling, or any otter from an otter polo team that has just lost a match.

This isn't to say that otters are wimpy by any means. Not every otter accepts the offered basic therapy after a traumatic experience and those that do have usually undergone several traumatic experiences. For instance, a losing otter polo team, already traumatized by the blows dealt during the game, is often set upon by fans of the winning team. This takes place after the game when the losing team is trying to leave the stadium, so a chase is usually involved, and most of these chases end in an accident and if the accident is a good one it's followed by any number of explosions.

That's three traumatic experiences for the losing otter polo team, and sometimes fans also chase down the medical vehicles that rush to the explosion, and so there's never a fixed number as to how many traumatic experiences that can be associated with an otter polo game, which is another one of the reasons it's so popular; the depth of its mystery.

In any case, when an otter feels particularly down, that otter can do basic therapy, which features Otkito, otter polo, fish, beavers, computers, loopeys, and goats.

Basic therapy is designed to rehabilitate an otter, to make that otter be an otter once again. It's a sequential system that begins simply, since most otters undergoing rehab are injured in one way or another, and the first step is days spent sitting in front row seats at otter polo matches.

OESG Note on Children: Totally helpless at birth and requiring decades of parental supervision, human children are generally the filthiest, loudest, worst behaved, most intellectually challenged and annoying members of the species, which also makes them the most entertaining.

Once the patient can move around, he or she is brought to a special center where there are beaver statues and a loopey. The first thing the otter does is practice art by painting circles as perfectly as possible on the beaver statues so that the loopey will throw its feces at it. Once a statue is hit 10 times, the otter is instructed in the correct manner for wiring the beaver statue with explosives. Then the statue is blown up.

Once nearly fully recovered, the otter is pitted against the robobeavers, which are robots that resemble beavers that are specifically designed to have a very small range of movement and be easily defeated. Using Otkito the otter is put to work destroying the robobeavers and then abandoning Otkito the otter takes a lance and is given a goat to ride, and then there is more fighting of robobeavers.

Also during rehab, the otter is supplied with the finest fish, and after a full course of basic therapy, an otter is unfailingly rejuvenated and ready to deal with the otter world once again.

As to the other types of therapy, they're really not worth explaining. For example, emotional therapy uses the exact same progression as basic therapy, but after each stage in the therapy, the otter writes down which emotions the event brought out. Likewise, for physical therapy, the basic therapy is used but with more accent on the Otkito exercises.

Therapy was what I needed after my day in the human world. At that point in my life, I had never undergone therapy simply because I considered it to be something for sissy otters. Once after a particularly violent otter polo match that my team lost, I was involved in 8 accidents and 6 explosions, besides the beating I received from the winning team's fans, and yet I refused basic therapy. I simply healed and went back into the world to exact the revenge I had spent that time planning.

After the stooges, the attempted kidney removal, the bag of air experience, being kicked in the butt by Vel and the storm, my otter resolve was low. If therapy were offered at that point in time on the bus, I would've undoubtedly accepted.

GOAT RIDER

The goat riding phase of basic therapy was drawn not from any historical goat riding in warfare, but from historical fiction that featured goat riding in warfare.

Then a child human strayed too close to me and I zapped the dirty little midget with my PHESA. When the child human jumped two feet into the air I felt my spirits rise. When I saw the child's hair standing straight up on its head, I began to laugh. When the little twerp ran to its mommy, I fell off my chair so strong was my amusement.

I actually cried at the beauty of the experience, and eagerly I stuck my head up to watch the aftermath of the shocking, but I didn't even look for the child because my eyes were locked onto something else out of the window.

As the bus slowed down to a halt, I felt a strong pull toward the vehicle's door. I quickly gave in and ran out of the bus. It wasn't the Como Zoo I had seen but something else entirely, and as usual, things went very, very wrong.

Sliding

What I had seen from the bus was obviously a water slide. That was the only purpose such a long chute with water running down it could serve, and as an otter, I was forced to investigate.

The use of water slides is one of the biggest social debates taking place on Revir. Ages ago, indeed back when we otters didn't possess technology or otter polo mallets, the preferred venues of recreation were water slides. The simple means of enjoyment occurred naturally alongside rivers and the otters of old divided their days between fishing and sliding.

They were happy, or we assume they were happy because there aren't any written records from that time, but all the old cave paintings invariably show two things: otters fishing, and otters sliding, so it's safe to assume that those two activities were at the time the two most important in daily otter life.

Sliding and fishing is the platform of the Return to Otter political party, or subversive group, depending on whom you ask. The group wishes for the return to the old ways, without all the trappings of modern technology and otter polo. They see the advances in our species as unnecessary burdens.

OTTER SLIDE

Their slogan is:
Technologies are unsafe bets
Bad computers and space rides
Otters carved the mallets
But the land made water slides

This group bases their creed on the most ancient of our stories, that of Vile Livinak, a young otter whose claim to fame is that he was the first to seriously be injured on a water slide. The story is an oral tradition that was handed down through tens of thousands of years before it was written down and anything worth retelling that many times is obviously a lie, but current scholars believe it's based on a shred of truth.

The story goes that Vile Livinak built a water slide down a mountain during the winter and awaited the spring thaw to use it. Unfortunately, which happens to be the very first 'unfortunately' in otter literature, Vile Livinak was an idiot, and because not all the snow and ice melted at the same time, he encountered several unkind bouncing situations during his descent without the luxury of a blowfish maneuver. Arriving at the bottom he was in a bad way, one might call it seriously injured, and Vile Livinak's mother had a fit.

Thus began the spurt in otter evolution. All over Revir the females banded together and outlawed the use of water slides. Of course, water slide use persisted in many areas, but in others where the females held sway the males got bored and found other things to do. Otter polo was discovered, or invented, and the next thousands of years were spent advancing the technologies of woodwork and medical care in order to make the game more enjoyable and survivable.

Suddenly the otter brains grew and the rest is all evolution history, but the water slides remained. A product of the natural world, no amount of civilizing could completely wash them away and no amount of potential scorn by a mother will stop an otterling from trying something potentially dangerous.

Thus the current water slide state has come, and for a time the ancient custom was regarded with the same respect and reverence we give to beavers, but then some smotter, which is short for schmuck otter and is the common term for all otters working for the government, took advantage of the Pack's establishment of a security force and actively went about punishing water slide use. It was just an excuse for his men to raise their slapping quotas, but before long they'd flooded Revir with so much propaganda about water slides that the next generation of otterlings was indoctrinated into a generation of water slide haters.

Of course, once those otters had otterlings those otterlings rebelled, and with more males succeeding in remaining unmarried well into their later years, many are reconsidering the wisdom of outlawing the water slides, like the Return to Otter members.

It is a complex issue, one of the most complex we otters deal with and any discussion of water slides eventually comes around to otter polo. Proponents of water slide legalization see otter polo as more destructive than water slides, while conservatives continue to cite the studies done years ago on the addictive effects of the water slide experience, but those same studies listed otter polo as even more addictive, and built a strong case for the opinion that water slides cause much fewer injuries and practically no explosions or riots.

Also controversial is the period of years during which otter polo was also banned. It was another condition imposed on us by the Pack after the beaver wars. They saw otter polo as barbaric, failing to see its inherent artistic aspects, and for a year, the otter polo players reverted to underground games and black market suppliers for the mallets. Also, there were no safety restrictions and otters began to weight their mallets with lead, leading to a huge spike in injuries.

And so that law was repealed, and all that could be done was done to make sure the wolves didn't find out. It wasn't very hard since the wolves find Revir offensive and never visit us, but it is something our diplomats have to keep lying about, and proponents of water slide legalization use the otter polo banning as an argument for legalizing water slides. With legalization and regulations, many of the accidents that currently take place could be avoided. Also, the excessive slapping admission for the secret water slides would drop.

Because water slides are still in use, they are as much of a part of life for many otters as otter polo was for me, and I don't want to say I've tried it, since such a confession might affect my career, but let's say that I've talked to otters that have tried it, and they enjoyed it immensely. The addictive effects, they claimed, were minor when the water slide was used in moderation, and on the whole, they found it to be less dangerous than even an amateur otter polo match.

I can't say who is right, but walking up to the human water slide park, I felt primal otter energy coursing through my body. I noticed the humans were paying money to enter, and I began again to question my theory of Three Stooge's addiction throughout the human world.

I wondered if perhaps the humans were addicted to several drugs or experiences, but then I noticed many of the parents were letting their children play without any real supervision so I concluded the water slide had nothing to do with addiction and was instead a troubling attempt at population control.

Staying clear of the ignorant child humans, I made my way up to the top of the slide. I looked down the chute of churning water and smooth plastic. I was at the precipice.

I tested with a toe and slipped.

Return to Otter

Down I went in the swirling thrust of liquid. I spun, I flipped and I bumped and bounced, and not once even considered doing a blowfish maneuver. At the end, I was shot out like the potato that struck my head while I was doing aerial circles with the jetpack. The panic barely had time to surface before I landed softly in a pool of water.

I was energized. I rushed from the pool and flew up the stairs, scrambling underneath the legs of the child humans. At the top once again I jumped head first down the slide and felt again the blistering exhilaration of the flow, winding my way once again to the pool below.

This continued for some time. I'm not sure exactly how long, but it was at least 5 hours, and I rationalized the detour of my mission by calling the experience necessary to my job as Head of Human Psychology, but nothing could have been further from the truth. I was simply feeling more alive than ever, more alive than when I had watched the Three Stooges. I had completely abandoned the guise of a seriously business-minded department head, and all rational thought had ceased.

Then I crashed into the pool one final time, and the waterproof capabilities of my PHESA became stretched beyond its limit. The Personal Handheld Electrical Shock Administrator shorted out, releasing all its energy into the pool of water, which conducts electricity remarkably well. My hair was quickly sticking straight out along with all the child humans in the pool. There were shrieks of surprise and pain, but not from me. I had handled a PHESA before and knew better than to stay in the vicinity of one that was shorted out.

I left the PHESA in the pool, ran a distance, and then turned to watch the level 1.834 self-destruct explosion empty the pool of water and child humans. It was an amazing sight; the exact opposite of what happens when a toilet is flushed. Child humans were scattered out of the pool and water drenched their on-looking parents. I was laughing until I noticed one of the child humans staring at me. I assumed the child was stunned and simply staring where I happened to be standing, but the child human's eyes had a creepy quality to them.

I sidestepped hoping to escape the child human's creepy stare, but the child human's creepy eyes followed me. Then the child human pointed and said, "Mommy look! Beaver!"

I braced myself to return the insult with a physical attack, but then I realized the creepy human child could see me. I checked my personal cloaking device and saw that it had been disabled by the PHESA discharge. I wondered what to do. Other humans were beginning to approach me.

Then the self-destruct on my personal cloaking device initiated and I was blown clear of the water slide park.

COMO ARRIVE

SPOCK IS AT ZE ZOO.

GOOD. IT'S TIME THIS ENDED.

Chapter 8

Zoo Landers

Reaching the downward end of my explosion driven journey in blowfish configuration, I came into a peculiar bouncing situation with a billboard, much like the advertisement for the Air Force that I crashed through.

This time, my flight was not due to a jetpack, and my momentum was nearly spent. Therefore, the bouncing situation wasn't actually a true bouncing situation, but a splatter one. A splatter situation is what happens when an object that has the ability to absorb shock is struck with a small amount of force by an object that does not recoil in the classic manner of a bouncing situation. Instead, the flying object flattens against the shock-absorbing object and remains there as if collated.

Being that I was in blowfish configuration, I should have rebounded from the billboard, but my air values had been strained the night before when the bag of air in the car struck me, and so when I struck the billboard my air valves let all my air out with the same telltale elephant farting sound.

Slowly, much as loopey mess slides off the red circle painted on the neighbor's door, I slid off the billboard and sunk to the ground.

When I regained the will to move my body I fell into the trap of baseball advertising, only in reverse. Just as when stuck with an object an otter has the tendency to examine that object, I looked at the object I had struck.

It read "Welcome to the Como Zoo."

Reading it, I sank back to the ground and curled up into a ball. I figured that since I had arrived at my destination I didn't need to rush finding Romeo. It was during this pained thinking that I had the idea that perhaps Romeo was no longer at the zoo, given the length of time between his arrival at the zoo and mine. This was a troubling thought. It meant that salvation might not exist beyond the doors to the animal show center.

This was not something good to think since it was mentally painful, and I was at that time in physical pain. The two should be handled separately, just as an otter polo player would make use of two mallets. No good can come from holding both mallets with one hand. Much better is to have one in each and perform either a whirlwind attack in which the bearer spins in the water and the striker only has to hold the mallets out, or a forking attack in which the striker aims one mallet at the enemy striker and the other at the enemy bearer beneath.

I'm getting off the subject. Basically, my mind was not helping alleviate my pain, so I put it to use fashioning a way to get inside the Zoo. I had no cloaking device, so I knew I would have to be secretive.

Once the pain subsided I set myself to looking forward to confronting Romeo if he happened to be in the zoo. I planned on being very forceful correcting his priorities, and planning violence is a good way to get an otter's mind thinking.

So there was the zoo, people entering the zoo for some show I assumed was starting soon, and I needed to get past the people and inside.

Before going on I should explain what I expected of the zoo. We otters have theaters that put on performances. Mostly they're just for snobby otters or snotters, but there are also the school plays the otterlings do, and those plays are seen as a form of art and treated with respect.

What happens is that an otter provides some spectacle, any spectacle, and if the crowd enjoys it they clap. If they don't like it they throw rocks and then the otter is forced to put on another spectacle by avoiding the rocks.

I assumed something roughly parallel happened at the zoo, although I had my doubts that rocks would be thrown. The dolphins and wolves have their own plays and rock throwing is not allowed, and at otter plays the audience brings their own rocks, whereas all the humans I saw were without rocks.

Nevertheless, I was hoping to see some good performances. I didn't delude myself into thinking that female Earth otters would be dancing erotically or anything on that order, but I was still hoping to see some excitement.

Getting back to the problem of getting inside the zoo, I first inspected it. There didn't seem to be a grand security system involved, only a wall that needed to be climbed. I was disappointed that the humans hadn't made better provisions for security but took advantage of their stupidity anyway.

Pulling air into my left leg and right arm, I achieved maximum-length span and pulled myself up to the top of the wall. There I discovered I had another problem. The wall had a roof on it, and I needed to get underneath the roof.

I walked around to find some way to access the down below. It wasn't long before I found what I assumed was an air vent. Ripping the covering grate off unceremoniously I squeezed inside and began to crawl into the tunnel.

At the end of the tunnel, I found that the air vent took a sharp turn to the down below. I fell, and just before I could perform a blowfish maneuver I broke through another grate and then fell several feet onto a dirt surface. This was another splatter situation.

I rose slowly from the ground and heard a low, guttural growling that I'd heard somewhere before. I thought about it, using my nearly photographic memory, and remembered it was during one of my discussions with Derbaron. He was talking about the beaver suits I seemed to recall. No, it wasn't the suits; it was the substitutes for the beavers he was explaining. He was playing the sounds of the various animals.

I turned and looked toward the growling, and discovered I was face to face with a Tasmanian Devil with an undoubtedly violent disposition. Our eyes met. Our bodies tensed. A fight ensued, and I discovered why Tasmanian Devils were rejected as sparing substitutes for beavers.

Well named, the little beast immediately tried to tear my head off. I dodged to the left and kicked with a well-timed slashing claw thrust. The blow didn't slow down the beast and only gave it my leg to bite.

For the next few minutes, I fought the devil off of my legs, which only worked because it began biting my right arm, working its way up to toward my head. I threw punches, I kicked, I slammed it against the bars, I even head-butted the vicious little mongrel, but it kept coming.

All the while I caught glimpses of child humans watching and giggling from behind a set of bars. It was these bars that eventually saved me. Freeing myself from those merciless jaws, I stood with my back to the bars. When the devil rushed again I dodged to the side. The mini beast smacked its head, and altering my body I squeezed out between the bars before the devil could recover.

I turned to sneer at him and found he wasn't looking at me, but was staring at my tail, which was still inside the cage. Latching on before I could remove it the devil caused the child humans to laugh again as it tried to pull me back through the bars by my tail.

Sacrificing some fur on my tail's tip I managed to get free of the demon's jaws. Breathing heavily, sweating, and shaking from fear of death, I ran for cover, pausing momentarily to snap my teeth at the child humans and send them running away screaming. Hiding behind a garbage receptacle, I took stock of myself. It looked as if I was suffering from the early stage of otter pattern baldness. My beautiful coat of fur was a mess with a few unsightly gaps where fur used to be. I was a terrible sight to behold.

Still safe for the moment I took stock of the area around me, wondering for the first time what condition of insanity would cause the humans to provide lodging to a Tasmanian Devil in Minnesota when I knew very well the species was not a native of the continent. What I saw, looking over the cages, bars, and animals, was very, very wrong.

Confrontation

The zoo, I discovered, was a prison. The animals were not performing; they were on display for human enjoyment.

Sickened with sadness, I tried not to believe it. Nothing like it existed anywhere else in the universe. It was a prison, not meant to punish, but to demean and prostitute other life forms by making them simple to find, robbing them of their mystery. The helpless beasts sat or walked behind their cages, looking at the humans watching them.

Sadness was everywhere. Coupled with pain was a lack of compassion, a lack of life. These animals were not living. They were dead, sterile and impotent. There was no compassion. It was if I dare use the word, inhumane, and yet it was uniquely a human innovation.

I watched in awe at the cruelty. Never in otter history had we considered such an establishment, such a concentration camp and if any otter had even dared to suggest something so barbaric it would have meant banishment to Nawiat for life.

"And the Pack thinks we're a menace," I hissed to myself, stepping out from behind the garbage receptacle to confront the human rat that was being led around by the child humans I'd scared off. He spotted me and rushed to grab me.

I held my ground, coldly breathing in rage and preparing. I tensed and pounced. I bit the man full force on the leg and held on. There was screaming and soon other humans were touching me. I continued to bite and to add to the effect I began to claw.

Finally, when I believed I'd made my point, I released my bite and put into use the classic otterling tactic of mother defense. Usually after destroying something belonging to another family, an otterling will run home and jump into its mother's arms. I did the same, curling up into a ball and doing my best to look cutely up at the human suddenly holding me, who happened to be female.

I watched as the humans relaxed into looking at me.

The man who I'd bitten tried to strike me with a blunt object. My new female protector protected me. "Don't!"

"Let me at him! He bit me!"

"Quiet!" With one lash of the tongue, the female quieted the human rat. "Tell me what happened, Earl."

"I dunno! God. That little monster just came at me."

"Look at him, the poor thing, he's all torn up. Where did you say the kids told you he was?"

"In there." Earl pointed at the cage with the devil. The devil noticed and hissed at me. I hissed back.

"He was in with the Taz? What was he doing in there? This is an otter! We don't keep otters with Tasmanian Devils."

"I don't see why not. That thing is a monster!"

"Well, what do you expect? He looks like he just went ten rounds with a Taz." The female proceeded to pet me. I allowed her. "You poor thing. He's all scared."

"Ah, c'mon. Quit babying that stupid animal."

Looking back at Earl with a sharp change in expression, the woman lashed again with her tongue in unmistakable rage. "I want to know what he was doing in there! Who's responsible for this? He could've been killed!"

The human rat stepped back. "It wasn't me!"

For the next several minutes I happily watched the display of a human female scolding the beaver flap out of a human male, who did not even appear to be her mate. I paid attention in case I was ever called upon to testify to the practical applications of sonic weaponry in human females and smiled repeatedly at the human male, which he noticed and sneered back only to in turn be noticed by the female who immediately increased the intensity of her scolding.

This sequence repeated the entire time I spent in their company and I heard it continue after we parted ways. The female was truly furious that I had somehow found my way into the Tasmanian Devil's cage whereas the man was totally convinced I was an untrustworthy creature while I was content to be cradled in the woman's arms while she scolded a man whom I had recently bitten.

After checking me carefully for serious injury, the humans brought me to another cage. I thought this was bad at first but then I realized that I was likely going to the otter cage, where I would likely find the female earth otter Romeo had deserted the Otternots to love, and of course Romeo himself.

Once inside I looked over the simple pool and rock landing, and it only took a second before my eyes locked onto exactly the otter I had been hoping to see. Across the small body of water was Romeo, the Head of Golfing Research.

Assembling all the anger I'd been storing up, I thought of all the evil in the human world that I had experienced, and I whispered softly, "There thou art, Romeo."

The Duel

There is a time for taking pause and reasoning out problems, but as a former otter polo player, I'm not inclined to notice those moments. With a renewed strength I dove into the water and shot out onto the rock where Romeo was relaxing with his female Earth otter. I wasn't even deterred by her beauty or attempt to greet me. I went past her and snapped into fighting stance. Out of reflex, Romeo did the same.

After a short stare down and exchange of taunts, I attacked with a Flying Fist and Claws Sandwich, in which I swung both my extended arms at him striking low with a fist with the left and the claws with the right up high. Romeo jumped from the fist, but the claws caught his legs and knocked him down.

With my opponent on the ground, I grabbed his tail and jerked him into the air and sent him back onto the ground with a tail body slam. Romeo recovered quickly and delivered foot taps to my belly and head. This hardly fazed me; such was my anger.

I fainted with a tail whip and actually struck with an upward back kick extension. I caught him in the soft spot underneath the chin, and this sent him into the air. I pressed to jump on him, but the female Earth otter came to his rescue with a flash of teeth and claws.

I dodged and blocked and kicked her in the head. No fancy move for it; it was a simple kick to the head that sent her sprawling toward the pool.

Seeing my mistreatment of his love Romeo let out a growl and sprung with a double claw dropkick, a fatal mistake. Using my superior skill I first balanced on my tail and then extended it so I was raised above Romeo's legs. As he passed underneath I struck down with all four limbs.

I put him down and kept him there with three limbs while with my right fist I gave him one calculated blow to the nose, which forced the back of his head into a bouncing situation with the rock below it, which knocked Romeo senseless.

Once Romeo was properly dazed and confused, I pulled him up on his feet by the ear and began slapping him, exacting payment for the suffering I had endured because of him as allowed by Otternot Disciplinary Code.

The slapping was vigorous continued for some time. I kept it up until Romeo began whining so badly that I knew his will was broken and he wouldn't give me any more problems.

"Owe!" Romeo cried, "Stop Spock! Owe! Owe!"

"Fine. Tell me," I demanded, "where's your shuttle?"

He pointed at the ceiling. "Up that air vent on the roof. There's a cloaked rope hanging over there. It's easy to find."

I slapped him for giving up the information so easily. "And all your stuff?" I asked, "Is it here or up there?"

"It's up there." I slapped him for effect. "It's up there! I swear!" I hit him again for swearing. "Owe! Quit hitting me!"

"All right. Now, I'm going to explain to you what's going to happen here, and I don't want to hear any backtalk."

Romeo pleaded, "Please don't take me away from her."

"Take you away? Oh no," I slapped him a last time, "You're not going anywhere." Then I kneed him in the reproductive area with a specialized technique that at the very least was sure to temporarily inhibit reproduction.

Finding the cloaked rope I climbed up to the roof and into the shuttle. After finding the survival kit inside I turned on the shuttle's computer. On the main screen, a picture of me appeared with a beanie hat. In reply, I held up the matter destabilizer I had taken from the shuttle's survival kit, and said, "Listen. I don't like you; you don't like me, but if you don't take me to the ship, I will gladly use this."

The picture of my face wearing the beanie promptly disappeared. The ship's engines started up. For a moment I relaxed at the familiar vibrations, thinking I had won, but then the engines went quiet and the picture of my face came back up on the screen, this time with overgrown beaver teeth.

Baring my pointy otter teeth, I aimed the matter destabilizer at the screen, squeezed the triggered and then suddenly had an idea. Leaving the shuttle I went back down to the zoo to get Romeo, having changed my mind about leaving him.

Chapter 9

Home Again

A short time later we returned to the Determined Goat 4, where I discovered I had attained celebrity status during my time away. Some of my otts from Natural Phenomenon Propagation had been hiding behind the grid of the air vent to the Man's office and heard him give me the mission. Also, one of Derbaron's underlings had blabbed about the whole thing because he works for the government and can't be fired.

Once the word was officially out Derbaron went to the trouble to distribute footage of my crashing into the Air Force billboard advertisement, and the entire crew had been viewing and enjoying my pain. Hearing that I was returning to the ship aboard the stolen shuttle, much of the crew assembled in the hanger to welcome me back by making fun of me, but then once again things went very very wrong.

Instead of laughter, I was greeted by screams of panic as the shuttle clipped the side of the hanger's open door and then crashed into a line of shuttles. The result is best described as chaos, with otters scrambling for cover while their uniforms inflated into space suits to protect them from the vacuum conditions after the hanger's air blew into outer space while lights were flickering and way too many sirens were blaring,

The crew had assembled to welcome me home as a hero but ended up attempting to physically beat me for scaring the beaver out of them, but I was in no mood for pleasantries or beatings, and I still had the matter destabilizer, which I was very close to using before the crew noticed the Earth ottay Elizabeth behind me inside the shuttle.

Seeing a live Earth ottay for the first time in their lives, the crew forgot all about the crash and me and started to compete for Elizabeth's attention, which annoyed Romeo. That's the last detail I remember before I was zapped unconscious once again by the ship's computer. I woke up in the debriefing room, shackled around the waist by a large clamp.

I had heard stories about the horrors of the debriefing room, but I had never before been in the clamp, which was what we called the waist shackle that prevented an otter from escaping before the debriefing was complete.

Most of the crew feared the clamp because they believed they could die of boredom if they talked about themselves for too long, but as the Head of Human Psychology I knew that wasn't true, and so I found my time in the clamp tedious but also somewhat therapeutic, probably because I got to complain about everything without any interruptions. I felt like I was working through some emotionally difficult stuff.

After however long it lasted, I finished my account of my adventure on Earth, which you're about to finish reading. I, of course, had to make a few edits to the original text, mostly so I could include what happened after I finished telling my story.

After I finished telling my story I remained in the clamp while the Man read my debriefing. I knew this because a screen was brought in the debriefing room so I could watch the Man while he read my debriefing, and I assume this was done as a punishment because I hadn't been scared of the clamp during the debriefing.

In less than five minutes I was bored to sleep, but every time my eyes closed the clamp would wake me up again by squeezing my waist enough that my eyes bulged a little out of their sockets. With increasing desperation I tried all of my stretching and air intake tricks only to fail to escape the clamp.

After hours of torture, the Man finished his reading and then spent the next hour discussing my story out loud with someone I either couldn't see or was imaginary.

Highlights from the Man's post-reading rant would be how angry he was that I named the Earth wolf after him, how angry he was about my chats with the human Vel, how deeply he doubted my assertions about the Three Stooges and how grimly he talked about the zoo.

Finished with his critique, the Man brought up a view of the debriefing room and saw me watching him. It took him a second to figure out that was what he was seeing, and then he demanded, "Beavers with wings, why is he watching me?"

No one answered that I could hear.

The Man yelled, "What is wrong with you? Turn it off!"

Final Trial

A short time later the clamp released me but before I could fall to the floor I was dressed in my old uniform and sucked up into the ship's tube network. A minute later I fell out of a tube into the conference room. Landing on the floor at a crouch, I refused for a moment to open my eyes and see what kind of a mess I had fallen into. Then I opened my eyes and found I was facing Gomer and surrounded by department heads.

Wary, I glanced around at the familiar faces, at Mikey Fish of Human Sociology, Gobbels of Human Abduction, Loki of Natural Phenomenon Propagation, Nester of Mythological Creature Propagation, Nero of Bird Behavior Altering, Pastor of Disease Manipulation, Aristole of Ozone Depletion, Nikititan of Ice Burg Placement, Ed of Computer Systems, Thorough of Earth Security, Calysapoc of Earthling Destruction, Windar of Primate Evolutional Studies, Poseidon of Weather System Supervision, Derbaron of Pilots, Sinoperag of Acoustic Amplification, and Heffner of Interplanetary Division of Inspection of Otter Terrestrials, who normally acts superior because his department's title is the longest, but was unusually humble just then because he was still recovering from injuries he sustained during the severe beating he received after the crew discovered he had been hiding Earth otter beauty from them.

After glancing around at the familiar faces, I remembered the misleading entries in the OESG and was about to lunge at Mikey Fish when the Man muttered, "Well Spock, I'd say you did a good job," and then went quiet.

Knowing the game the Man was playing, I smiled, bowed and then played along by saying, "Thank-."

"But you didn't!" The Man interrupted, slamming a paw to the floor. "I should banish you to the beaver planet for this!"

I replied defiantly, "Well then it's a good thing you can't."

Frowning, the Man asked, "Don't you know that beaver planet is another name for the deepest level of the brig?"

"Oh cmon," I complained, "You read the story? Haven't I suffered enough already? And why is it wrong to say that I did a good job? I got the job done, didn't I? That's good enough, isn't it? Well if it's good enough then it's also good," I argued, "That's basic math, good plus is greater than and partially equal to good alone, so," I nodded, "I did do a good job."

Sputtering a laugh, the Man asked, "You think your Human Psychology word tricks can save you now? While I'm sitting here with this," he pulled out a long sheet of paper from behind his back, "list of your violations, which I had to print out because I knew I couldn't remember them all?"

"That's all taken out of my debriefing," I said pointing at the Man, "You can't use that. You tortured me to get it, and I was probably lying. That thing is at least," I shrugged, "oh, I 'd say it's about... upper forty percent misinformation."

"Oh, upper forty," the Man scoffed, "That low?"

"It's under fifty," I claimed, "It has to be, because while I was on Earth I acted completely within the bounds of all applicable Otternot regulations, for somewhere around about almost most of the time, maybe," I shrugged, "But regardless of whatever that means, you should let me off easy on this."

The Man teased, "Should I? Let the record show the accused would prefer not to punished for his crimes."

"That's a great idea," I said loudly, "Way better an idea than this stupid trial, or whatever it is you're doing. Cause this," I insisted, "is a waste of our time. There's no winner here. We all loe. It's just sad really. It makes me think of... sadness."

Pointing at his list, the Man replied, "This should make you sad. You should be ashamed. It's disgraceful."

"Whatever. That's just your opinion and you just happen to be in charge. That doesn't mean you always get your way."

"Perhaps," the Man said pointed down, "but most of the time can still include this point in time."

I warned him, "You don't want to do this, Gomer. Trust me on this," I nodded, "This is a bad deal. You should let it go."

"Noted," the Man grumbled unimpressed as he looked down at his list, "I trust my opinion. Now, item number one."

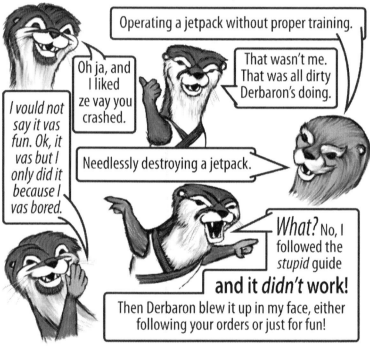

The Man continued, "Using a matter destabilizer without proper training and without just cause-."

"Just cause?" I interrupted. "I was totally justified."

"You evaporated a defenseless human structure, now quit interrupting! Let's see.. multiple counts of using a neural destabilizer... causing a human aircraft to crash."

I objected, "The helicopter was an honest accident."

The Man wondered, "And how about the children you assaulted with a PHESA? Was that accidental?"

"I think," I replied, "that was... educational. Yeah! It's like a kind of survival training. Making them wiser about life."

"Oh," the Man said neutrally, "Really? And what exactly did you teach them by using a PHESA on them while you were cloaked? Was that your way of teaching them to detect cloaked otters, because it looks like simple sadism to me?"

"To a layman maybe, but I believe it could be a vital skill for a human," I half agreed sidestepping with my Head of Human Psychology skill, "but the real question isn't if I did this or if this was or if it wasn't because as otters our way is forward, and to get there we have to start here and there's no point in looking back because we'll only move forward as well as we can keep in the here and now because that's where the truth has to be heard, my otts. Here and now is the only place truth is found and that's what should be our priority here, not making someone a villain. No, we don't need that,

because that's the very thing that we otter not be doing, just look at us all, wasting time with the past. It's tragic."

203

Interesting, but tell me, did I forget to mention that Derbaron followed you everywere recording everything you did?

No, I didn't know about that until just now. Curse you Derbaron.

Getting back to the list, assaulting a mime with a neural destabilizer, a crime of dispassion I suppose you'll claim, and a juggler, and causing dozens of cars accidents.

Those roads are deathtraps. You go cross a street and then judge me.

Laziness is what that was. Talking to a human without using a neural desta-bilizer afterward, explaining dinosaur extinction to a human, Atlantis, the chocolate eucalyptus etc. diet, using Otkito techniques on a human, disguis-ing yourself as a human, biting a human. I mean c'mon Spock, you placed yourself by word into a rank below that of a beaver during an intelligence comparison. That's a clear violation of the foremost rule of otter honor.

I was fighting for my life, and what is this? A Pack Inquisition? I completed my stupid mission! I didn't want it, but I did it and that means all this is really your fault! You should've known better than to send someone with a bad atti-tude like mine down there. I should sue you for incompetent leadership.

The Man asked, "Care to confess anything else?"

Smiling, I asked, "Am I under arrest then?"

The Man nodded vigorously. "Oh yes. Very much so."

"Then I get to send a message."

Looking puzzled, the Man asked. "So what? So you get a message. Who do you think you know that can help you?"

"Well, I'd like to send a note to the Pack. I'm wondering what they'd think about human subjugating Earth wolves and their zoo prison. I think the Pack would be very interested."

The room was quiet enough to hear a weasel scampering. The Man glared at me and then looked around at the department heads. I had him, and he knew it.

The Man's only real job was to make sure the secrets of Earth stayed secret from the Pack. If my message went through, there very quickly would not be an Earth to supply Revir with the entertainment it had grown accustomed to having, and that would trigger a revolution which would mean the Man would lose his pension.

Not only did I have blackmail material to hold over his head, so did every other department head on the ship. For a minute, the Man sat thinking, and then his shoulders sank in what I assumed to be defeat, but then he looked up with bright eyes and a gleaming smile. I worried I might be in trouble.

"Spock," the Man said warmly, "I think you're right."

I wasn't deceived by the fake admission of my superiority because I knew the no good Man was up to something else. I asked slowly, "Right... about... what... exactly?"

"About everything. You've proven yourself to be the best otter on this ship." The Man smiled wider and looked around the room for approval of the statement from the department heads. None came, and the Man asked with an angry tone, "Don't you all think so?"

A round of approval came from the department heads, all the heads except for me. I was beginning to catch onto the Man's game. "Wait a sec-."

"No Spock, don't be humble," the Man dismissed, "You've done a good job, and you shall be rewarded. I promote you to Captain and give you command of this ship."

A gasp went over the room. It wasn't only due to surprise, but also out of wonder at the Man's ingenious ploy. With all the blackmail material floating around the ship, the job of the Captain would be harder than ever. By making me Captain the Man could retire, and while he got away from it all at the same time I would be punished greatly by being forced to do a job I would loath.

"No!" I yelled, throwing out my only defense, working one of the loopholes of the Otternot regulations. "You can't! I resign my position as Head of Human Psychology!"

By Otternot Law a promotion must be processed to be valid, while a resignation once given is immediate in effect, and since I was a department head and not part of the ship's government crew I had a right to resign at will.

"Accepted," the Man said with a laugh of triumph, "I accept, and before all department heads I use my authority as Captain of the Determined Goat 4 to conscript you into the Otternots for 30 years without possibility of early discharge. I promote you to the rank of Captain, name you my successor and then," he smiled as wide as he possibly could, "I resign."

The ship's computer listened constantly for such orders and recorded all high-level meetings so we could go back and hear the actual words said after one fight or another had broken out because of those said words, so while the Man and I parried with our given powers, the computer had been keeping track and waiting for the situation to be decided.

At the moment the Man said he resigned, a computer voice chimed, "Resignation of Captain Gomer confirmed. Now evaluating all queued orders. Evaluation complete. Command of the Determined Goat 4 transferred to new recruit Captain Spock. Revir update sent. Awaiting new orders."

The Man stood, stretched his neck, blew air across his claws and then walked for the door. Without a pause, he removed the ceremonial ruby fish necklace and threw it up into the air so it landed perfectly in front of me. Still without looking back, the former Man laughed, "The ship's all yours, Captain Spock," and then exited through the door.

Without the former Man, I looked around at the other

equally stunned department heads.

"Yowzah," Loki exclaimed, "He up and done beaver slapped you something fierce, Spock."

I bristled, "Go chase minnows, Loki."

Loki smiled and saluted. "Whatever you say, Cap."

I crumbled my face into my hands. "Curse the beavers, how did I not see this coming!"

"All you otterlings should keep in mind," Sinoperag, the senior department head of the ship, told us all, "it is not by being a beaver that one becomes the Man."

We all looked at him, I more crossly than the others.

"Unless your name is Spock," added Mikey Fish.

The collected department heads laughed at me while I wallowed more snugly into the depths of misery. Then I heard the voice of Bodawk, the ship's spiritual adviser. He said, "There is a proverb better suited for this moment. There's a few actually, but the only one I can remember right now is the secret to good cheer is taking the fun at hand."

As the words sank in I reached the bottom of my self-pity and then began to rise back to the surface. Then I realized I was in charge of the ship, and whatever the hassles of being the Man there would also undoubtedly be perks I would enjoy.

I promptly cheered up a great deal. Looking around at my crew, I wondered what to have them do first. I remembered my plan to abduct the Three Stooges but decided to start with something simpler. After a moment searching for a suitable first task as the Man, I ordered the department heads, "Alright you lazy no goods, get busy cleaning this ship with your tails!"

That's how I became the Man.

I CAN UNDERSTAND WHY SOMEONE ELSE WOULD FIND THAT IDEA INTERESTING BUT UNTIL YOU COMPLETE YOUR ORIENTATION AND HAVE YOUR COMMAND OF THIS SHIP CONFIRMED, YOU WON'T BE GIVING ANY ORDERS, ACTING CAPTAIN SPOCK.

Acting Captain? And what does that make you then, a rude piece of jewelry? You scared the beaver out of me talking like that, you dirty... whatever you are.

I WILL EXPLAIN ALL THE DETAILS DURING THE RETURN TRIP TO REVIR FOR YOUR ORIENTATION.

Revir? That's a great idea. Hey is that your job? Helping me, like some kinda talking pet sidekick?

NO. I AM THE COMPUTER RUNNING THIS SHIP, AND NOW I WILL RUN YOU TOO.

TO BE CONTINUED IN *OTTERNOT 2: REVIR RUN*

AUTHOR BIO

The author posing with fish (smallmouth bass?) he caught in the BWCA (Boundary Waters Canoe Area).*

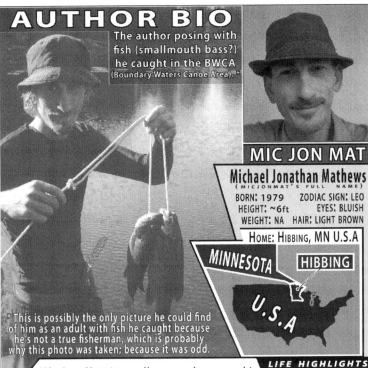

MIC JON MAT

Michael Jonathan Mathews
(MICJONMAT'S FULL NAME)

BORN: 1979   ZODIAC SIGN: LEO
HEIGHT: ~6ft   EYES: BLUISH
WEIGHT: NA   HAIR: LIGHT BROWN

HOME: HIBBING, MN U.S.A

MINNESOTA   HIBBING

U.S.A

* This is possibly the only picture he could find of him as an adult with fish he caught because he's not a true fisherman, which is probably why this photo was taken; because it was odd.

Mic Jon Mat is usually somewhere near his hometown Hibbing on the Iron Range in the northeast of Minnesota, where he has spent most of his time since 2001 after abandoning a career in computer technology to pursue a less stable and profitable career writing fiction in the tradition of starving artists through the ages but using the tools of the Digital Age, resulting in hopefully less starving.

LIFE HIGHLIGHTS

PEDALLED A BICYCLE ACROSS USA
(WEST TO EAST, NORTH TO SOUTH)
BILINGUAL ENGLISH/FRENCH
(SPANISH, GERMAN, JAPANESE)
GOOD   FAIR   ANIME
DANCES IN PUBLIC WHILE SOBER
LIVED IN FRANCE (1997-98)
ROLLER DERBY REFEREE
HACKY SACK MASTER
COMPUTER LITERATE
SURVIVED BRACES

For even more information on Mic Jon Mat or to help fund his adventures by purchasing his stories, go to:

MICJONMAT.COM

or find him on Facebook, look for this logo